# Dustland

# ODYSSEY

# Dustland

## VIRGINIA HAMILTON

An Odyssey Book
Harcourt Brace Jovanovich, Publishers
San Diego   New York   London

Requests for permission to make copies of any part of the work
should be mailed to: Greenwillow Books, a division of William
Morrow & Company, Inc., 105 Madison Avenue, New York,
New York 10016.

Library of Congress Cataloging-in-Publication Data
Hamilton, Virginia.
Dustland/Virginia Hamilton.
p.    cm.
"An Odyssey book."
Summary: Four children, all possessing extraordinary mental
powers, are projected far into the future to a bleak region called
Dustland. A sequel to "Justice and Her Brothers."
ISBN 0-15-224315-1
[1. Time travel — Fiction. 2. Extrasensory perception — Fiction.
3. Fantasy.] I. Title.
PZ7.H1828Du    1989
[Fic] — dc20          89-7591

Printed in the United States of America
First HBJ/Odyssey edition
A B C D E

For my sisters
Barbara Davis and Nina Anthony

# 1

The unit hummed. It had the power of four. It was Thomas, the magician. It was Dorian, the healer. It was Justice, who was the Watcher and the balance for the unit's strength. And it was Levi, brother of Justice and identical brother of Thomas. Levi suffered for them all.

This was the second day that the unit had been out of its own time and into the future. Its first day had been uneventful; yet it had been a frightful day. Because, in its first attempt at mind-jumping, the unit appeared to have traveled into a place of endless, gritty dust. It could distinguish no landmarks. It saw no growth, no animals, no humans. But it divined instantly what must be the scarcest commodity if such a land were inhabited. It named the place Dustland.

The unit directed. It sensed a wellfield seventy feet below Dustland's surface. Using its mind as a vector, it willed and jetted the underground water in a stream to the top of the dust. The water collected into an impure half-acre pool. The Watcher and the healer drained off some of the impurities while Thomas and Levi focused its energy, keeping it steady. Watcher and healer drew pollutants into themselves and cast them out again. As the process continued, the two, Justice and Dorian, appeared to creep and ooze.

Presently the unit's work was finished. Justice and Dorian took on semblances of themselves as the single rhythm of the unit shut down. They and Thomas and Levi breathed individually and saw individually as the Watcher faded from their eyes.

"Let me test the water," said Thomas. At once a goblet was in his hand.

It was quite pretty, Justice thought, made as it was of glass trimmed in gold. It was Thomas' joke. Being a magician, he could cause anything to appear out of thin air. But of course the goblet would never hold water, since it was only air shaped and formed by magic.

Playfully, Thomas dipped the goblet in the pool. He had clouded their minds completely so that they saw exactly what he wanted them to see, at least for a few seconds. Justice was amazed when the goblet filled with water; it had to be part of the illusion Thomas had created. Yet she sensed that it wasn't, although it came to her that Thomas would think that it was.

What's going on here? she wondered.

The magic goblet faded and water dribbled through Thomas' fingers.

He drank from his cupped hands. "Whew! That's still rank," he said, making a face. "But it's good and cold. Sweet, for making it cold, Dorian."

Thomas said *sweet* for the things he thought were cool or tough. But he hadn't thanked Justice, even though she and the healer had cleansed and freshened the pool together. Part of his disregard for her she knew was because she was only eleven while he, Levi and Dorian were thirteen. And she was the only girl.

Thomas and Levi, being identical and inseparable, had known of each other's extrasensory ability since childhood. Justice had known of her superior powers only this year and with the help of Dorian and his mother, the Sensitive. But from the beginning Thomas had suspected she had the power. And he had shown often enough through the years that he never liked her. Now the array of extrasensory she had could offset the combined force of the others—Thomas, Dorian, Levi and even that of the Sensitive. It was she who had formed them into a unit so that they could mind-jump to the future.

"A person over there has to be joined," Justice

had once told Thomas. "There's no other way to survive."

Thomas had sworn he would never become part of a unit. A monster-machine, he called it, controlled by her.

But they had become the first unit under her direction. And Thomas had built up enough grudging malice against her to do her harm if somehow he found a way to overcome her.

Their first trip to the future ended after the second day. They created the pool and cleansed it. They had heard no unusual sounds, had seen nothing beyond the dust. With a feeling of letdown, they joined into the unit and mind-jumped back to their own time.

A few days later the four of them made a second trip to Dustland and they came upon a marvelous creature.

They were again the unit. The unit had passed through the Crossover between past and future. It had concentrated its energy on the one certainty it had—Dustland. The Watcher had protected it through, surrounding it with its immense force. The unit materialized in the putrid place, where all was the same murkiness of dust. The Watcher faded from them and they were again their separate selves.

"It's Dustland, all right," Dorian said. He was a thin boy, but wiry and strong.

"Isn't it fantastic?" Justice said. "We can jump whenever we want to."

"So what if we can?" Thomas said. "Who wants to come to this stinking hole?"

"Come on, Tom-Tom," said Levi. "This is the same place, but it might be a different part of it."

"Well, who cares?" Thomas said. "If this is the future, you can have it, buddy. There's not a bloody thing here but dust."

He was wrong. They had not been long in Dustland when they became aware of a creature galloping across the wasteland.

Justice homed in her telepathy on the four-legged creature. She did not enter the creature's mind, but trailed along a stream of thoughts and fragments as the creature ran. It was female, and totally at one with Dustland.

This land, in which graygrowth is eaten cleanly below the dust, was a fragment with which Justice's mind collided. She telepathed to the others to scan her mind as she observed the creature. The others scanned her and knew what she knew.

Hordes passing over the same ground.

Hordes of what? Thomas wondered.

Hordes, human groups, passing over the same ground as the creature.

The she-one did not know where the hordes

were going or if ever the same returned. She did not care. Galloping, she scented a Dawip and raced ahead of it to intercept it.

A Dawip? Dorian wondered.

Justice gave them an image of a small animal, quite fleshy. It was prime food for the she-one and a delicacy. The fleshy little beast had the misfortune to have hopped into the creature's range.

The she-one leaped in a spectacular flight through the air for a distance of twenty feet. She landed on the little beast, trapping it between her paws, and broke its neck in the process.

*Let's get closer*, Justice traced in the minds of Thomas, Levi and Dorian.

They came nearer, close enough to hear the sounds the she-one made as she ate the Dawip's delicate ears. Next she stripped away thin skin and striped back fur with her tongue and front teeth. As the Dawip's blood seeped through tissues, she lapped it up. It was the first clean moisture she had had in weeks. Finally the creature ate, holding herself back from gulping the tiny beast in two bites.

Justice revealed to the others that the creature was aware of them. Thomas had opened the strange corridor between his and his brother's minds so that Levi could *see* as Thomas did. For Levi could not mind-read on his own. Then all four of them homed in on the creature's thinking.

She was aware only that she was being watched. She made no movement that might warn them she knew they were there. She sat in the dust, carefully licking the Dawip's bones. She thought of hiding the small skeleton in the earth, to have tasty bones within her reach. But a sense of all things being even came to her. She would leave the bones lying about. Let starving hordes find them and use them to season their mudsip. If the bones were added to the graygrowth of flat, stringy threads that sprouted just below the dust, the hordes would survive.

The creature was posed regally, with the bones trapped between her paws. She stared at nothing. Occasionally she blinked her enormous eyes; pointed her wide, leafy ears. There were orange membrane pouches behind the ears that swelled and pulsated.

Aware she was that she was being watched; yet she saw no one. There were forms, shapes, hardly thicker than gritty air that had come very close to her. Lines came to her, around the shapes. The shapes filled and she sensed colors washing down over the shapes. Forms were similar to humans but taller than any she had ever come upon.

*It senses us*, Justice traced. *With bodies and with clothes, just as we do, when we know we can't have our bodies with us!*

*Maybe it's a condition of Dustland that you*

*have to have bodies*, Levi traced. *And if you come here with just your mind, it'll provide the body for you.*

*But how does Dustland know to make the body look like yours or mine?* The question hung on the air.

The creature was *hearing* their mental tracings. She gathered impressions of their thoughts, which were like imprints. The imprints did not come quite clear to her understanding. Not at first; but then more so.

*She's beautiful, isn't she?* was the shape of one imprint pressed on her mind.

That had come from Justice.

*But what is she?* traced Dorian.

The she-one was beginning to comprehend the tracings.

*I don't know what she is,* Justice traced. *She looks kind of like a bear, doesn't she? But smaller.*

*No, she's more like a dog, a mastiff of some kind, but bigger,* traced Dorian. *Much bigger. Have you ever seen a dog with those . . . those ear-bag things?*

They stared at her. They were thinking to one another about her. Still there were some imprints she didn't understand. *Dog. Bear.* Words about things she had no knowledge of.

*Does it breathe through those bag things, you*

*think?* Levi traced. The imprint hit the creature like a soothing voice.

*Well, they move in and out, sort of like breathing*, Thomas traced, interested in spite of himself. *Look, I think we should move back. We're too close and we don't know what she might do.*

Calmly the she-one listened in on them, aware of many imprints. She was alert. Quite ready to attack.

*Don't get so close to it!* Thomas traced.

*Not it, her*, Justice traced. *If she wanted to start something, she probably would have by now. She knows we're here. Besides, she can't hurt us.*

*Don't be so sure*, Thomas traced. *We don't know much of anything yet. I'm not even sure it's the same time period as the last time.*

"It's the same. I know that, if nothing else," Justice said. She decided to talk softly, since nothing they did seemed to disturb the creature. "And we can't be hurt," Justice added. "Because, if we were, we wouldn't be the same in the past, would we?"

"I don't figure that at all," Thomas said. He was talking as softly as Justice had. "If hurt here, we're hurt at home."

"But that can't be," she said. "If hurt here, it hasn't happened, and it cannot happen in the past. It never will happen."

9

"Oh, I don't know!" Thomas muttered. "I don't know *anything*. But I can feel the grit on my skin. I get hungry and I get thirsty when all I have is my mind here. I'm getting myself scared, so, please, let's go back home!"

"I can't do that," she said.

He knew there was no arguing with her, and it made him more bitter, more angry than ever.

Justice was excited over their discovery. "Can you just imagine the odds of us finding anything out here so soon?" she said. "I mean, I would've guessed we might find something in a month, maybe. But you can never tell about chance."

"That animal right there could be the only thing here," Levi said.

The she-one sensed a hand lifting and pointing at her. In her mind there was an explosion of fear.

"What if she's some beast out of the past and not the future?" Dorian asked.

"There was never an animal like her in our past," Levi said.

"But there was something like it," Justice said.

"There was?" Dorian said.

"Yes, but it didn't have the pouches. I've seen pictures, I remember—what scientists think the first canine might've looked like. It ate meat, too, forty million years before our present."

"You know that for sure?" Thomas said.

"Well, would I lie to you? I read all about it,"

Justice said. "And the canine was called . . . Miacis."

"Miacis!" Levi said.

"Hey, Miacis!" Dorian called. "Here, girl! Miacis, come!"

The human forms moved about. They were unlike any the she-one had sensed before. Their mouths moved, uttering sounds. They touched hands together, causing loud and sharp reports that hurt her hearing.

Her withers trembled above her shoulders. The third eyelid of her glowing eyes swept across the transparent corneas and cleansed them of dust. Her ears stood to their full width as her hearing tuned sharply higher.

She was aware. The first time ever being called. Miacis. Miacis! A wondrous sound, as though—she was aware—she had wanted the name and had waited each Nolight and Graylight to have it. Hearing *Miacis* over and over, she felt about to roll around at the feet of the human forms so different from any others.

She held herself back. Caution was the wisdom of the she-one, now called Miacis, and the reason she was healthy and remained uninjured.

But she was also aware. She listened to the name she accepted as hers. She followed the talking from one human to another. Did not move one muscle that this kind would notice. Through her senses, she knew their size. They were larger than she in some ways. They were bigger and straighter than any others of humankind. She scented a wonderful healthiness about them. Miacis watched them, calculating their combined strength.

"But you know, really," Levi said, "this could be the past."

"Because of that thing there?" Thomas said. "Not bloody likely. Not with pouches like that. And take a look at the stuff on the ground. Ashes, or something like that. It smells of chemicals. Probably it's poisonous."

"I don't smell anything," Dorian said.

"Well, I do! Maybe everything was leveled in some big disaster," Thomas said.

*Chem-chem . . . dis-aster?*

The humans stood absolutely still, observed Miacis.

"Who . . . who was that?" Thomas whispered.

"Well, it wasn't me," Justice said.

"Me neither," said Dorian.

"Levi, was it you?" asked Justice. "Did you catch it? It said *disaster*, and it was trying to say *chemical*, I think."

"Maybe it was random," Levi said. Random was feedback. Unconnected words.

Miacis was aware of this. She discovered she could imprint her own thought to them. She had questioned *disaster*. But the forms were not answering her. She did not like the feeling they gave her.

She extended the well-developed dewclaws of her forefeet. They were like slender thumbs with razor-sharp nails. Her great fangs were hidden beneath the heavy sag of her hips. The fangs throbbed with cold feeling. She desired blood, and gathered herself in.

But something happened. One of the humans came to a hair's-breadth away from her. She could feel its energy.

"Don't be afraid," gently it spoke. It touched Miacis' head in the center, above the eyes. It moved its hand up and down.

Never had Miacis known human touch. She had not ever dreamed of such a thing. No one had touched her.

"Huum?" the human said. "You like being petted like this? Miacis? You like that name?" It stroked her fur above the ears. "I am the Watcher," it said. "But you can call me Justice." It laughed, baring teeth.

Part of Miacis would bite off the touching hand in one swipe of her incisors. Taste blood and suck the bones! But another part of her felt a glow. She spread her forepaws and embraced the kneeling human. Heard it gasp as she caught it in and held it firmly by the arms.

"Stay back!" Justice warned the others, who had moved to protect her.

"But it has you trapped," Levi said. "It's got hold of you!"

"Levi, she can't hurt me. We're not really here, remember?"

"You don't know that yet," Thomas said. "So what's it got there, if it isn't you?"

Miacis had hold of the human called Justice. Justice quaked in her grasp and Miacis loosened her hold, but not enough for Justice to get away.

Justice stroked her fur and stared into her eyes. "You're some kind of great one, I'm sure of it," she said. "I think I'll make you my partner in this expedition."

Miacis suspected some trick. Yet she thoroughly enjoyed the stroking.

Justice closed her eyes and leaned her head against Miacis' jaw.

Such a one!

She rubbed her forehead against Miacis' cheek and wrapped her arms about Miacis' neck.

Miacis aware suddenly that the human was a she-child. Aware also of the warm human arm against her air membrane. She nuzzled the dark curls on the child's soft, tender neck.

Such a young one, so plump with flesh! Not scrawny and strong-smelling like all the others. Miacis need only turn her head slightly, bare her teeth and sink mighty incisors through human skin, flesh and bone. One bite to break the neck clean, and the head from the spine.

Ahhhh.

Miacis licked the young-one's neck, where she discovered hairs much like fuzzy fur.

Justice shuddered.

Miacis waited. If the child attempted to escape, Miacis would stun it by inserting her poisonous dewclaws into the soft arms as she held them. But there was no need for any attack. The young-one had begun mind-tracing, with Miacis hardly aware that the tracing had started.

Justice closed her eyes, resting her hand on Miacis' head. The hand grew heavy. By using her hand, she was able to make Miacis see and feel. Miacis saw and scented an unheard-of loveliness. Places beyond imagining. Words whose meanings she now understood. How green and wild-scented was *grass* with *clover! Barns—a backyard*. The *hedgerow!* Words were like tender Dawip bones.

Miacis understood that the humans could become a unit. The unit wished to exchange knowledge with Miacis. It, through the Watcher, informed Miacis of much and asked many questions. The unit sensed that its destiny depended on the survival of others in Miacis' realm. It worried that it did not know who these others might be. It had found no humans yet. It sensed something wrong, but did not know what that was. It sensed that it had some design, some mission, but had no knowledge of what that was, either.

Miacis trembled. She had never known such power from so few who called themselves a unit. She feared the unit might trap her. She released the human, Justice of first contact, and backed away.

No one tried to stop her as she trotted off as though leaving for good. She circled back and found the four parts of the unit as she had left them. There came gentle probes into her mind from the Justice one who had petted her and named her. These were attempts to free her from her apprehension. But Miacis used her own mental strength and managed to brush the probes aside. She wouldn't allow contact with Justice again. Each time the she-child wove a thought, Miacis trotted away. Only when left alone would Miacis veer and return.

The encounter lasted for some time. Miacis circled, setting up sense-posts to surround the unit. But the force from the unit dissolved them. She didn't know whether to run away or stay at a safe distance. She began chasing her long, luxuriant tail—what was she to do? She became dizzy and fell awkwardly in the dust.

The four laughed at her, smacking their hands together.

Such loud noise hurt, like hard blows. Miacis sprang from a crouch and attacked. She flew through the air at Justice and landed on her, hard. The impact should have knocked the she-child to the ground. Instead, Miacis passed right through her. There was no Justice. There was nothing beneath Miacis' paws.

The rest of them were still. With a ferocious growl, Miacis hurled herself upon them. She slashed with her deadly dewclaws and caught the humans off guard. She struck, and felt triumphant pleasure as she came in contact with solid weight. But her forefeet passed through air. Exactly as before, there was nothing whatever for her to sink her teeth into. She hit the ground with awful force. Howled in pain.

Justice held her hands out to Miacis, walking slowly around her. Miacis found that she had no further desire to attack Justice or any of them. She was awed.

"See?" Justice said to the others. "We can't be harmed here."

Thomas looked doubtful, but said nothing.

Justice touched Miacis between the eyes. And, recognizing the touch, Miacis allowed it again.

*Poor Miacis*, Justice traced. *You need a friend, I'll be your friend. We'll be friends together.*

Miacis bowed her head. All fear and ferocity evaporated from her. *I am with you, master.*

*I'm not your master. I'm not anyone's master,* Justice traced. *Where'd you get that idea? I am the Watcher, a friend come to visit.*

Miacis knew nothing of friendship. She was aware of something dark of the mind. She knew master and its opposite. If she could not bring down this one human part of a unit of four parts, if she could not tear it in pieces beyond its use for anything but food, then she, Miacis, had to be slave.

Soon the Master was teaching her how to bring down a prey, which she already knew well enough how to do. But the Master taught her to bring the prey back to her uninjured, something Miacis had not known how to do.

So it was that Miacis knew herself to be slave. She did not mind. If the Master wished not to be called by the name *Master*, then Miacis was obliged to obey. But now Miacis' steady vision of the chance meeting between herself and the unit had shown clearly that the Watcher, Justice, was the Master of Miacis.

Miacis now found a new state of peace. Having the Master made her ever more content.

# 2

___

"We have many like you at home," Justice said to Miacis. "People keep them as pets."

*People?* Miacis questioned.

"Humans," Justice said.

*What are pets?* Miacis traced.

The unit had gone back to its own time, and now it had returned. This was its third journey to Dustland and its first day back. It had found Miacis waiting for it by the pool. It soon discovered the animal's remarkable ability to learn its language from the thoughts and speech of the four.

Now Justice chattered conversationally. She traced in the mind only when it was easier or necessary to do so. She was telling Miacis that pets were friends to humans. "Companions to play with and hunt with," she said. "Maybe dogs to protect people and their property. And seeing-eye dogs to be the sight for the blind."

This last caused Miacis' fur to bristle, for she

was almost totally blind herself. At once she was aware that the Master knew she could not see. Coldly, Miacis turned away.

*I hunt not for others*, she stroked in the mind of the Master, Justice. *I do not play with human groups. I will not be guard for them! I am the only. I am Miacis, alone.* She held her head high. But she did not mention or even think to herself that there was someone else, for fear the Master would read it. There was someone for Miacis. There was Star.

Justice continued, "Miacis is an olden name, that's why I gave it to you. Because there's a chance you might be a throwback to that ancient breed. But you can't be the single one left. There were so many dogs and wolves all through time. Every one of them except you couldn't have died out."

*Many, my Master? On my life, there are no others like me. There are cutting and fighting beasts like me with four legs. Perhaps they are your . . . dogs. None are as strong, as swift and keen as Miacis.*

"I bet none of them can mind-trace the way you do, either," Justice said.

Miacis turned her head away. She was aware that probably she had always been able to mind-trace but had had no one to trace with until now. What she could not do was voice-talk, and that upset her. She wanted a sound, clear and high, like the Master's; and a rippling laughter, too. Immediately she began to study how such sound was made.

They were all at rest beside the pool the unit had created. Justice sat with her arm around Miacis' neck, stroking her golden fur. Levi and Dorian were watching the pool with undivided attention. And Thomas was off on the other side, studying creatures Miacis called worlmas and examining them with some of his tools.

The pool was full of creatures like none they'd ever seen. Miacis would not trouble her mind to identify such lowly creatures other than the worlmas with stick-like, pencil-thin legs.

Earlier in the day Thomas had discovered that he could make sharp tools by hewing bones he found in the compacted earth beneath the dust. Wandering groups snatched up most of the bones to mix with their mudsip gruel, so the unit had learned from Miacis. With Levi helping him, Thomas rubbed the bones he found with gritty dust. Even Miacis had been made to help in the new craft of bone-sharpening. But, clearly, she was a reluctant worker.

"This stuff could take the paint off a Ford Mustang," Thomas said about the dust. He instructed Miacis, "Chew this end of the bone until it's pointed. Well, do the best you can with the point, dog. Scrape this one until it shreds. I need about five bones shredded into claws."

Miacis would do as she'd been told only after Justice told Thomas never to call her *dog* again and after Justice said it was all right for her to work for Thomas. But after chewing and scraping the bones. Miacis slunk away. She had moaned her displeasure, her orange pouches swelling and surging.

It was now early afternoon, in Justice's judgment of the time, and bullet-shaped worlmas were all over the place. Many creatures had drowned in the pool, but worlmas were sucking in the water. They began growing from an average size of a garden snail to that of a fist.

Thomas wanted to kill the worlmas straightaway. But Justice wanted to find out how much water they could hold. She wondered what would happen to the worlmas' spindly legs under so much sudden weight. The worlmas' legs weren't growing at the same rate as their bodies.

"Their bodies may not be stretching at all," Justice said. "The water could be causing some chemical change, making the cells multiply."

"Who cares?" Thomas said. But they all watched, fascinated, as an overweight worlma struggled out of the pool. It tried to crawl away, only to have its legs snap in three places with a sound like corn popping.

"You look like you're going to puke!" Thomas said to Levi, who had covered his eyes.

Brownish liquid trickled from the breaks in the worlma's legs.

*Healer, here's your chance,* Justice traced to Dorian. *That thing is probably in pain.*

"Forget it, Healer," Thomas said, mind-reading them. Before anybody could move, he had taken his sharpest bone and slashed the worlma down its back. There was a tiny sound like a faraway horn: *pank-a pank!* The worlma collapsed in a gush of its insides that stained the dust brown.

"Did you hear that?" Thomas said, laughing. "It goes off every time you try to waste one of 'em."

Justice and Dorian rushed to the creature. "Is there life still?" Justice said.

Dorian nodded.

"Then try," she said.

He lifted both hands above the broken worlma. Minutes later, what rose weakly from the dust was a normal-size worlma on stick legs. It was shaky, but it was healed.

"Wonderful," Justice whispered.

"It would've died," Dorian told Thomas. "Too much growing has changed the balance. They can't take what pollutants are left in the pool. You don't need to kill them."

"Oh, cheezus!" Thomas said, exasperated. "That's all you know, buddy. Them things would

*2 3*

die even without some pollutants. You wanna know why? Because they're made wrong, that's why."

"What?" Justice said. Miacis purred evenly against her arm, her blazing eyes staring at Thomas.

"What I said," said Thomas, "is that they are made *wrong*. I've been combing their insides and I know how they work. I know that they get choked on the dust and they die. Oh, they don't have throats that choke. But the dust oozes in through their skin and it chokes up their workings and they die."

"I haven't seen any of them die!" Levi said.

"Well, maybe you haven't been looking hard enough," Thomas told him. "Because they *do* die, and all the time, too. But they don't *stop* to die."

Dorian and Levi stared at him. Miacis blinked.

"Give him a chance to explain," Justice said, before either of them could say anything.

"Well, thanks, girl," Thomas said. "Glad somebody around here cares to listen some."

Always as sarcastic as he can be, thought Justice.

They were silent, watching the creatures. Worlmas in the water grew to ten times their original size. They floated like footballs made too large. And when they tried to leave the pool, their legs broke under the pressure of their overblown bodies.

"Brother!" Justice cried. "How big would they get if they had an ocean to swim in?"

"There'd have to be a point where growth reached its outer limit," Dorian said.

"That could be at the size of an elephant," Levi said, "depending on the quantity and purity of the water."

"So, as I was saying," Thomas began, "these beasties don't know when they've kicked the bucket. You can't tell dead ones from live ones walking around unless you have something like a sharp knife. Then you slit one down its back. If the brown stain flows, it's alive and it dies. You slit another one and what happens? Whatever life was in there, the mucous stuff, the membranes and the brown-stain acids, whatever," Thomas said, "it's gone, or drying up. But the beastie keeps right on moving until it's so dried up it breaks apart into small pieces, which break up into even smaller pieces. But it never will go *pank-a-pank*! unless that brown stuff flows."

"You sure of that?" Levi said, the sound of alarm in his voice.

"Positive," said Thomas, proud of his scientific study of worlmas. "I'm telling you. They ought to die right off, all at once, but they don't. Because these buggers are programmed to move around so they can dry out. Once they're all dry, they come apart in littler and littler pieces. No remains to clutter up the place. All very efficient. It's in the genetic code for beasties, I'd say."

"So the dust is . . ." Levi began.

". . . is maybe everything that has to die here," Thomas finished for him. "I thought of that, too. That's if moving around after death, drying up and falling to dust, is the same code for everything. But we don't know that, either. Moving around after death could be an involuntary action, kind of like a slow rigor mortis." He glanced at Justice and quickly away.

He had been looking at her fast and sideways like that all day, Justice realized.

"I don't like any of it, much. It's creepy," Dorian said.

"To think things can be moving around and dead at the same time," Levi said solemnly. "You see them and you don't even know they're dead."

"But how long do they keep on moving?" Dorian wanted to know.

"It would depend on the genetic code for the kind you're talking about," Thomas explained.

"So how long does a worlma move around after death?" Levi asked.

"I can't say for sure. It could be an hour or a day dead. Probably no more than two, three days dead to dry up and pull apart. But I'm guessing."

Silence, in which they watched creatures

struggle and die. In which Justice closed off a tracing between her and Miacis so the others couldn't scan.

*Talking about worlmas, Master, shoot,* Miacis tracing. Her language was a mixture of words she found in any of their minds. *Worlmas ain't no nevermind to nothing, man, lady. He hiding something?* This about Thomas.

Justice had to laugh, but kept it within. *Thomas gets interested in something, he won't let it go,* she traced.

"We going to sit around here forever?" Thomas said, suddenly impatient with small creatures.

"Where do you want to go?" Justice asked him smoothly. She was a study in relaxation, stroking the golden animal at her side.

"Well, don't you have a plan or something? You brought us here."

She smiled at him. "The plan is to stay right here by the water. Everything, whatever kinds there are, has to have water and will come here eventually."

"Yeah, eat us and then drink!"

"Oh, for heaven sakes, Thomas," she said. "We can't be eaten or hurt here."

"Don't you believe it," he said quietly, controlling his anger. "And I don't like it out in the open like this. We should become the unit."

"Don't we always become the unit, Thomas?"

"Yeah, but not soon enough. We should become it before Nolight."

Thought he hated the unit, she thought, making sure she kept it to herself.

"We'll have the unit when Nolight comes," she said.

*Not far off now, my Master*, Miacis traced.

*Please, call me Justice*, Justice traced back, automatically now, she had traced the same thing so many times.

*Yes, Master*, traced Miacis.

Justice sighed, patted the animal; then pushed her away and lay down, leaning on her elbows.

"Meanwhile," Thomas said, "think I'll make me something. I don't care for being out here like sitting ducks."

The next moment the four of them and Miacis were positioned high on a cliff edge. Gleaming white rock had fallen from the face of the cliff, rising nearly as high as the cliff itself.

"Oh!" cried Justice, lifting her feet away from the dangerous edge. Miacis switched her marvelous tail, but otherwise made no move.

Thomas laughed. Far below them and all around was Dustland with its endless sameness. "How you like that?" Thomas asked them.

"Neat!" said Dorian.

They all had the sensation that they were at

the very top of a cliff, when actually they were still in the open on the dusty ground. And nothing coming anywhere near them would be able to see them. All that was visible was the real pool and the shining rock and cliff of Thomas' powerful magic.

"I'm getting dizzy way up here," Dorian said.

"Sweet, isn't it?" Thomas asked, looking at Justice.

She had to admit that it was. "Guess it *is* better that we not stay in the open," she said, "even with the unit."

When, later, the landscape began changing in glowing shades that reddened the dust, they knew the sun was going down. One instant there was still Graylight; the next, there was the darkness of the period Miacis called Nolight.

Nolight was more oppressive than any nighttime at home. For one thing, it felt heavy. With the dust, it sifted the day's heat down on the unit so that the power of four could think of nothing else. The unit grew vague and listless as the rhythms of this strange place relaxed it overmuch. Only one of the four kept all his wits about him.

Thomas violently wrenched himself out of the unit, tearing away psychic chunks of the rest of them as he did so. Justice, Dorian and Levi were rendered unconscious, with only Miacis to watch over them.

The golden animal had lain between Justice and Levi. She had not bothered to cover herself with dust this Nolight, as was her way. With the Master beside her, she had no fear of the open. She neither believed nor disbelieved that Thomas' cliff hid them all, for, being blind, she couldn't see how craftily the illusion was erected. Then, suddenly, three sleeping humans had started up in awful, convulsive movements and fallen back. As Thomas pulled away, Miacis rose on her four legs.

"You come near me, dog-face," Thomas whispered, "and I'll carve you in little pieces." He had the bone-claw weapons that Miacis had bitten and chewed to razor sharpness.

Miacis stared in Thomas' direction. She sensed how strange was this one, who called himself human. Proudly she sat down again, swishing her tail.

*Going somewhere, are you, buddy?* she traced to Thomas.

The sentences Miacis was able to put together from words out of his own mind shocked him. Yet he wasn't going to let their slangy accuracy throw him now.

*You stay back, dog-face. Yeah. I'm going someplace. She thinks she can run me. Either she leaves me be or I'll stay out there and none of them will ever get home. You tell her that, dog. Tell Justice I don't*

*want to come here ever again! And if she wants to
get back home, she'd better make some promises!*

*Sure, what's your game?* Miacis traced.
*Brother, you are some tough guy for sure.*

She turned clear around so that her back was
to him. She flicked her gorgeous tail at him just
once. But before she turned, she had sensed something. Thomas was concealing something behind
him—some form, some shape. Without having
seen it, she knew it was important.

*That's okay, man,* Miacis traced. *You get yourself a good headstart.*

*Come after me, I'll slice you up!* warned
Thomas. He was already running, putting distance
between them.

Justice came to with Miacis licking her face.
She had a terrible headache and hurt all over. She
knew at once what had happened. Thomas. He
was gone, of course.

"Why didn't you wake me?" she demanded of
Miacis.

*I waited for you to awaken, Master,* traced
Miacis.

"Then why didn't you stop him if you were
awake when he ran?" Justice demanded.

*The Master didn't command me to,* traced Miacis. *I was resting. Think I must've been sleeping,
oh, yes.*

"Well, which?" Justice said angrily. "Or was

it all three?" She got up to see about Dorian and Levi. Dorian was coming out of it as if from an uncomfortable, cramping sleep. Levi lay still, breathing softly.

She returned to Miacis. "Answer me!"

*I . . . saw him leave. But I couldn't go after him till you told me to, Master. But you tell me to and I'll bring him on in. You just let me at him, oh, yes!*

Justice said nothing for a moment as she scanned Miacis' thoughts.

"So that's why you didn't try to wake me," Justice said, probing. "You wanted to give him a good headstart. Why, you love a run, a good chase! What's going on between you two? I bet he wants you to chase him, doesn't he?"

"You want me to wake Levi?" Dorian said, interrupting them.

"No," Justice said. "Give him time. He'll come out of it like we did."

"Why did he do it?" Dorian asked, speaking of Thomas.

"Part of it's to get back at me," Justice said. "And then, he's planning some game on Miacis, I suspect. But mainly he hates coming here, so he's showing me that none of us can get back home until he says so."

*He say you better promise to stay home for good, too,* Miacis traced.

"Oh, he did, did he?" Justice said.

*I can bring him back, Master. Let me go get him.*

"I ought to go myself," Justice said. She glanced apprehensively over at Levi.

"I don't get it," Dorian said. "How can he run away when . . . when nothing of any of us is here to run?"

"I don't know," she said. "But just look at us." She was wearing a hooded robe and sandals. Dorian and Levi had on hooded tunics with pants that fitted tightly about the ankles. "There's some unknown affecting things. Thomas did run away and we've got to get him back."

She looked over at Levi and knew she couldn't leave him. She would need Dorian, the healer, if Levi was deeply hurt. Only time would tell.

Justice turned to Miacis, not quite sure she had made up her mind. But Miacis was aware she had.

*Thank you, Master!* Miacis leaped away. In seconds she was streaking across the Nolight of Dustland.

"Wait!" Justice called. But Miacis was gone.

How can Miacis bring him back? Justice wondered. Rarely now did she think of Miacis as an animal. She was rather more like a cousin. And she divined that somehow Miacis could do what she set out to do.

*We can't get home. Bring him back!*

# 3

Miacis growled. She was impatient to complete her task for her Master as soon as possible. But fast motion always gave her so much pleasure.

Softly, she growled again, enjoying the thought of the capture to come. Perhaps she should run even faster in order to get the long pursuit over with. At top speed she could gallop, streaking across the dust.

Make capture before another Nolight, she thought. Maybe. But surely I would suffer the heat, and collapse out here all alone.

Miacis had the sense to hold herself in. She trotted southward on the course she had been on since she'd taken off in Nolight. Graylight was still some time-distance off. Steadily she closed the gap between herself and Thomas, the prey.

Miacis set her mind free to range ahead, scanning objects at a great distance which were hidden from ordinary sight. Soon she made contact with something that leaped in her mind. It shimmered there as with a strong pulse. Miacis homed in on the prey without Thomas ever knowing.

In the high heat of dismal light, she lowered the level of her energy and slowed down. She was aware that others came into her range. Off to her left, she sensed a group moving in her direction. Their shallow, confused thoughts—fears, mostly— flowed over her like a bad odor.

Will they never learn to keep their minds to themselves? she wondered. She reached out to give them a thought or two of her own.

*Do not approach*, she mind-traced to them. *Nothing is here for you. Death and hunger be on my course. I am Miacis and I do not lie.*

She heaved her massive chest, proud of her formal mind-talk. She knew the group would obey her anyway, but she did enjoy having them know that her name was Miacis. When she howled at them, the group turned. With their last strength, they moved off in a run.

She was not cruel. She did not hate these help- less groups. Some creatures known as Slakers Mia- cis did despise, but not these groups of poor, weakling humans. And now she telepathed to them what she knew: *Once I have passed out of range, head across my trail. I saw yallows not far off. Dig beneath in the shadow of the surface vine to the roots. You humans, suck the roots.*

Human minds recoiled from hers. *Poison!* They feared making deep contact with so powerful an animal. *Poison!*

*Not poison, not,* Miacis traced, as simply as she knew how. *Make hurt you in arm and knee bends. But not kill you. Very nourishment. Humans, suck yallow root. True thought from Miacis.*

She was aware that some groups were more alert than others, the kind that knew to fear her. These were such a group. They waited until she had passed far beyond them before they moved again.

Ranging, ever ranging, it seemed to Miacis that her hind and fore feet no longer touched the ground. Even the hip and back aching that came with a long pursuit had worked itself out of her system. She felt wonderful moving with her easy grace. Knew how she must look, with muscles so loose and smooth they made hardly a ripple under her burnished fur. Her fur turned a dark orange-yellow when she had meat. But most often she ate graygrowth for months at a time; her coat would seem a deeper hue as she licked it.

Thoughts of the prey returned to her. Her mind might stray, but it would quickly return to the pursuit. The prey would surely be half dead by the time she reached him. And half starved.

Likely, she thought, he'll scream cursing at

me. He'll not take warmfood I cast up for him from my own stomach. Such a one!

Part of her mind concentrated on the range far ahead around the prey. She allowed that part to measure the drag of the prey's exhaustion. For the first time on this pursuit, she let it probe, sliding up Thomas' back and into his brain.

The prey convulsed with fear. As if hit with a club, Thomas was struck with the knowledge that Miacis was with him. He knew now, for sure, that she had tracked him down.

Miacis touched along the prey's pain centers. She suggested to him that he quit his futile attempt to outrun her and give up.

*Take the route of least suffering,* she traced to him. *Let Miacis take you back as fast as I can.*

But the prey also had power. Thomas ripped her probe to shreds and flung it back at her. He had bound the shreds in his deepest feelings, flinging the sorrowing bundle at her before she could properly shield against it. Miacis bowed down under the pressure of his terrible longing for home. For the first time, she felt sympathy for the prey.

Was not she free to range as she pleased? Even though she knew a master, the Watcher, was not she still free to be where she liked?

Thomas traced in her mind: *As long as you stick around Justice, you're caught by the Watcher the same as me. You don't know it, but you're never going to be free again.*

Thomas' mind-signal had come like a feeble whisper on fading strength.

She was touched by the prey's longing.

She trotted lightly, her huge ears held high, which made thought transference from a mind such as the prey's much easier.

*You'll have to take me,* traced the prey. *I'm ready for you. I'll not give up. I still have my weapons.*

Miacis whined. She panted, then clamped her muzzle shut. She wouldn't allow herself to think to the prey and risk having him see into her plans. Trotting faster, she noticed that she raised dust with each step, for it tickled her nostrils. She made no sound.

She was aware. Distinguishing the slight but steady rise of land by the heightened tone of her muscles and the gradual changing of the dustland to a more rocky terrain. All around her like a second coat over her fur was the absolute darkness of the land. There was no brownscape. No tinges of red of fading Star. For Star had gone and would come again only with Graylight.

She was aware. She talked to Star, but had never seen It. Aware that her coatfur color and the color of Star were often the same intensity. Behind all in Dustland was Star. When Nolight was near, Star began to fade. Finally It slept, as now—as Miacis would have, save for the chase. All things slept; even the Master, Justice. But the Master with her unit did mostly as she pleased.

The terrain now revealed boulders and broken slabs of rock. Even in the dullness the boulders glinted, for they were made smooth and shiny by ferocious, gritty Roller storms. The Rollers came without warning. They came vivid with lightstreaks and rolling noise. They did not frighten Miacis. It was by means of them that she was delivered unto Star.

Living beings sensed it was best to stay out of Miacis' territory. The trouble was, she changed her territory at will. Groups in her path had no sense of her power unless she let them know it. Only her discipline kept her from cutting a part from its group, knocking it down and stunning it with poison from her dewclaws. With the drug paralyzing it, Miacis would begin nibbling at it and end by feasting on it. But such meals were rare for her because of their side-effects. Awful dreams came as she lay digesting. Graylights of waking with an urgent tail-pounding as she lolled stupidly. Only hours later was she able to heave herself up, feeling weak, tail aching, and with an awful taste in her mouth.

Miacis ceased trotting and scanned the area around her for a *dark*. To her right was an outcropping of rock. She sensed along its rise, up and up into gritty Nolight.

A good place beneath the rock, she thought, feeling somewhat tired herself. A good, safe *dark*.

She glided over there, panting slightly. Tiny tremors flowed down her back into her legs. She was aware and sensed that all was well around her. Soon she was burrowing into cool dust at the base of the rock. Under the surface she hit dry dirt and began digging with hard, strong thrusts of her back and front paws.

Digging was never easy work, but within what the Master called half-hour she had made a *dark* to a good, safe depth. Exhausted now, she crawled in on her stomach and twisted over onto her back. She worked her hindquarters, pushing and scraping with her paws until she had dirt and dust covering her over. Only her muzzle and lip were left uncovered to the Nolight. The bright orange membrane behind each of her ears that separated dust and monoxide from the air she breathed, she kept covered completely. She was aware that, even when she was worn out, the membrane glowed, revealing her hiding hole. With the membranes closed, she sucked air through her nose and began using her undeveloped lungs as breathing organs for as long as she was at rest.

Lying on her back the way she was, she would have been open to attack if she had not concealed herself so well. She was aware of her bulk and heaviness in her cramped quarters; but she was totally invisible in her *dark*.

Miacis was huge for an animal of her realm and larger than any of the human groups, save for Slakers.

But what are Slakers? They are nothing, she thought.

She weighed more than two hundred pounds, so the Master estimated. Yet she remained alone, with no unit, out here in the open. Therefore she had to hide herself well from any who might pass her way and attempt to trap her.

Fear. Miacis knew it. She feared being trapped, although, as far as she could reckon, she never had been. But once confined, she realized, there would be no one to come to her rescue. There were no others of her kind anywhere in Dustland. She had told Star this fact, but had not found the courage to ask Star to do anything for her.

And Star has done nothing, she thought. Perhaps it is not Its place to. Oh, but now my Master would come if I were trapped, she thought. I know she would! The Master would search and search for me. She would find me and lead me to safety.

To the Master, Miacis admitted she could barely see. She was aware that her near-blindness had always been so. Yet she noticed forms, shapes, the instant they moved. She could recognize Star color, and natural growth by scent; and rock, landrise and fall by telepathic second sight. She and the Master kept her lack of first sight their secret. The Master teaching that if the prey, Thomas, discovered her blindness, he might find a way to hurt her.

*Not me*, Miacis had traced to the Master. *He come near me, I feel it all over. Sock that buddy down, too, oh, yes!*

"Miacis, you won't hurt anyone," Justice had told her. "I'm telling you not to."

So the Master had spoken to Miacis.

Oh, wish I could go home with the Master, too! Miacis thought now.

But she was of this place the Master called the future. The Master and the others were of the place called past. None of them could enter the future alone. The four entered the future as a unit only. And Miacis could not ever enter the past. In the past, she had not existed.

She had been so informed by the Master. And the Master called herself human and called the other three human. Miacis knew better than that. She knew humans of her land. She was aware that the Master was like Star and was greater than all others. Was glorious.

Master might be Star in disguise. Find out how good I be.

Miacis knew of good and bad from the unit. She cared nothing about them, but she would try caring in case the Master was indeed Star.

Concealed in her *dark*, Miacis thrilled at being so informed about so much by her Master. Slowly she relaxed her bulk in the tight place. She had a single sense-stream, like a fluttering ribbon of sensation, connected to the feelings of Thomas, the prey. She would loosen the ribbon, pulling it back, as soon as he fell asleep. She allowed herself a moment of emotion so that she might be touched by the prey's desires.

She was aware. Thomas shivered with cold, although the Nolight was stifling.

*Dig*, Miacis traced along the sense-stream. *Dig in the dust. Your body losing moisture. Exposure will cause fever. Nothing lives in the open. The open will shorten your flight and the chase unduly.*

Thomas marveling at her knowledge of his slightest discomfort. This came to her along the sense-stream. He was furious that she should attempt to help him. And there was wonderment from him at the vastness of Dustland. Its dismal emptiness, he called it.

Not so, thought Miacis.

What's happened? It was the question that wove in and out of Thomas' mind, even when he was thinking about something else. This question and other thoughts flowed back along the sense-stream to Miacis.

Where are the trees? came from him.

*What are trees?* Miacis tracing, telepathing. The prey refused her question. Then she remembered Justice showing pictures of the past and the *hedgerow* of trees.

Has there been a war? Thomas was wondering. *What is war?*

This . . . this awful, fantastic, smelly dust—is it a season? He wondered. Will things change and grow? Where are all the people? Where are the cities? What kind of place is this?

*I know cities.* Why did she say that? Once she had told Justice she knew cities, too. Why did she lie? She didn't know or care.

But the prey had traced the thought. *You know cities? Miacis!* Tracing to her. She had got his attention for sure. *Then where are they? Why didn't you tell us, Miacis? Justice said there were no structures here.*

*The Master is truly right*, traced Miacis. *What are cities? There are no cities. Now, please dig in the ground. You know what little fighting beasts will do to you if they find you. Oh, but I leave from knowing. You are not here, Thomas, the prey, not really here. Not in what is body, is that not so? I cannot keep it straight. Nothing like you,*

*the unit, has occurred here. You seem . . . real. I
have sensed . . . seen you move through the space
around you. Seen you move objects. I have come
in contact with your weight. Therefore you are here,
are you not?*

*Dustcreep!* traced Thomas, the prey. She felt
him pull his forces in from her. He raised mental
shields, hiding himself. *Good night, Dustshit,* he
traced evenly.

*Whatever is good night?* she traced. She had
heard and scanned his curses before and had a
growing collection she kept to herself.

*I'll not teach you anything, you stinking dust-
keeper!* And then: *You'll never catch me.*

In this way, the prey signed off for the remaining time of Nolight.

Miacis moaned and sighed. So insulting he was
to her. Dustkeeper! His last jape at her before he
covered himself over with dust and dirt and fell
into a deep slumber. It took him time to dig his
*dark*—he made it very wide (Ha! thought Miacis,
I wonder!)—and it took him time to settle in. But
at last, with his retreat from her, she emptied her
mind of his feeling and loosened and pulled back
the sense-stream. So good to be no longer connected to the prey's mournful pain and loneliness.
Yet she moaned continually at his breaking all
contact with her and his lack of caution in the
Nolight.

From her cramped position in the *dark*, she set up sense-posts around the prey to protect him and give herself warning. The sense-posts would cause her hindquarters to tingle uncomfortably in the event something disturbed the prey's *dark*.

He may not be like Star. He may truly be of the past, thought Miacis. But he can be found here and now. He can be sniffed by beasts of Nolight who grope, unseen, to hurt him.

Tiredness reached into the marrow of her bones. Her breath came in rushes of awkward lung-breathing. Each time she exhaled, a high whine left her throat. It was a thin sound which gave her satisfaction, reminding her of the pleasure she found on the edge of sleep.

Tired to my teeth, as the prey would say, Miacis thought. She sighed. The prey do carry on such cursing, too! Funny stuff!

She snuggled deeper. Images drifted in and out of her mind. Breathing grainy air, she was aware of no disturbance. Sensed no Rollers on the borders of Nolight. This she knew of Rollers. They were her ships; she, their herald. This she accepted.

Whining, Miacis fell in and out of an agitated surface sleep as through frightening emptiness. Within vague dreaming, she asked herself, "Is my Master touching me? Who is here?"

She slept, dreaming. Hers was the land. Its sameness was happiness.

The dreaming changed. She searched for creatures and could not find them. Saw herself, whining and forlorn, futilely hunting. Star-glow spoke to her that, once touched by humans, she would never be the same again.

Then this changed. Peace came. It was the Master.

Miacis warm now in her *darkden*. Her breath came in shallow puffs. She was now deep asleep. No dreams to see. Stillness within. But much later she again was aware.

Miacis sprang loose from the *dark*. Before she was wide awake, she commenced galloping in long, powerful pulls of her legs.

Almost Graylight, she thought. Man, brother! I sure was sleeping—damn!

Her sense-posts around the prey had been numbed. All but one, that is, which the prey had overlooked. That single sense-post had managed an uncomfortable tremor deep within her. It was what had awakened her.

The prey was on the move. How long he'd been going, Miacis couldn't say. But he was moving fast.

# 4

Justice imaged huge. Twelve feet tall, she moved slowly, aimlessly, back and forth, before she settled down at last in billows of choking dust. Awesome she was as she bent on one leg and rested foot-wide hands on her right knee. Her gaze seared furrows in Dustland ground.

Abruptly, Justice quit it. She tuned herself down to conserve her and the healer's power.

Since Thomas' escape, Levi had been only semi-conscious, lying in the dust. She thought it best to leave him as he was.

Give him more time, she thought. He's bound to come out of it the way we did. It just takes him longer because he's not as strong.

Larger than anyone in real life back home, Justice breathed in waves that stirred the grimy powder at her feet into ebb and flow.

"Better to be huge, like me," she rumbled, just to hear how scary was her roar and mutter.

Dorian trembled at the sputtering echoes her voice made.

"Better being large than little-bitty, teeny-tiny!" she growled at the murk of Dustland. "Really bad news being the size of some dripping germ-o!"

After the shadowy day of Graylight had come, Justice had made herself as minute as a bacterium. Being microscopic had taken what seemed a life-time. Years, in which she fought a creature who tried to trap her in the sticky substance dribbling from slits in its face. She had used her will on it. And the creature had brought others to surround her and catch her off guard.

"That's no fair!" she yelled at them. "You have to fight me one at a time!"

But they would not. They forced her to invent something—a deadly piece made from Dustland's grime and sub-atomic grit. The weapon had done the job. It sliced through germs cleanly. Forced to kill in self-defense, well, then, best that the dirty work be done smoothly, was Justice's opin-ion. Before imaging large once again, she'd bal-anced the weapon on her thumb for a last good look at it. What a gleam it had!

Now she kept the weapon safe in the crease her thumb made, in that line above the joint. There was an immense chasm for hiding anything so minute as her deadly weapon. If she should need to image tiny again, the weapon would be instantly in her palm.

Dorian peered up at her. He didn't speak to her or shake his head at her. There wasn't any need to. She read him without altering her tired gaze from the land. If she stayed large, she would soon sap him of his healer's power.

The two of them weren't as close as they would have been had the unit stayed whole. But they held together some part of the enormous sensation that was the unit's power. Desperately they needed Thomas in order to have the unit again. Justice and the healer were bound in understanding. Their minds had made the same connections. They had seen the same since the time back home when Justice learned of her power through Dorian and his mother, the Sensitive.

Now she imaged normal height and size. Dorian settled next to her. His mental aura calmed her.

"Only reason I made myself grow was to forget the pain," she told him. "I feel like I have a hundred muscle cramps from doing handstands all day."

"It's not true pain," he told her.

"Well, it sure feels like it," she said.

"When Thomas pulled out," Dorian said, "he took psychic chunks of us with him."

"But I can feel aching in my arms and legs just like it was real," she said.

The healer placed his hand on her brow. At once her spirits lifted. Her discomfort moved up and out, as though through the top of her head.

"Don't hurt yourself," she told him. Dorian took on others' pain as though it were his own. Soon her distress faded out of his eyes. His expression relaxed.

"You must be a god, Healer," she said.

He smiled. She had made him smile for the first time this day. "It's the unit that's the god," softly he spoke. "Sometimes it scares me. And you must be the Goddess Enormous." He managed a grin at her, but, clearly, his heart wasn't in it. Dustland always made him uneasy.

"No, but really," she said, "can't you grow up and down the way I do?"

"I haven't tried," he said. "Remember, you only just sprung it on me awhile ago. But I know I can't do it."

"It's part of me in the past and the part of me here combining, projecting huge and then tiny," she said. "I hate tiny. I don't know why I do it. All those slimy buggies. Guess they're part of the future, too, but who can tell? Yuk!"

Dorian laughed. "You sound just like some little eleven-year-old."

"Which I am," she said, "way back in the world before Dustland." To think about home made her sad and teary-eyed.

"Your mind is growing beyond us," the healer said. "We'll never be able to keep up, the rest of us won't."

"Don't say that," she said. She didn't like being separate from them because of her greater power. Studying her friend, she wondered if some-day when they grew up they would marry. She allowed Dorian to become alert to her thinking. He mind-read her and blushed.

"I was only kidding," she said kindly. "But we'll always be close friends, won't we?" And he nodded his agreement.

Both of them were made edgy by Thomas' run-ning away, by Levi's long sleep and by the strange-ness of Dustland. They wanted to be back home; but they couldn't get there without Thomas. And they concentrated on keeping their growing fear at bay.

That was the reason they sought a mutual cen-ter. The healer closed his eyes. Justice had already done so. They formed themselves in dusky shade beside the deep, inner current of themselves. They gazed in at the still center. It gave back only their reflection, at first. Then it brought home to them.

Justice's father and mother in the front parlor of their home. All was in disarray. Mrs. Douglass sat with hands clutching her arms, her head bowed. Mr. Douglass sat across from her. He leaned forward as if about to say something to her, something for which he could never quite find the words. Their faces sagged with fatigue more than age. Their eyes glinted with the pain of anger, insult. Fear. Emotions came on and went off, like blinking lights through wet window glass.

Justice ached inside to see her folks so miserable.

"They haven't changed," Dorian spoke within. "You suppose if my mom stopped over there the next time, it would ease them a little?"

"Nothing much can ease them," Justice said. "We've all tried. Nothing will change their minds about us. Oh, let's look at home the way it used to be. I liked it better then."

They saw scenes, not the way home was now, now that it had become a heartache for Justice. They saw it the way it had been when only they and Dorian's mother knew of their power.

Dorian felt a longing, then, for the past, as Justice did.

Houses of their small town, windows open and window screens in place. Light spilling out of the windows in bright squares on black lawns. It was a hot summer night at home and there were spearmint breezes blowing. Lightning bugs were sparks in the dark fields.

They, all of Justice's family, were outside. Dorian was there, too. He was as close to family as he could be. Even Thomas was there. And Levi. Justice's mom and dad, too. Mr. Douglass picked tomatoes in the dark. Had a paper sack to put them in. The sack crackled every time he carefully placed a tomato in it. Made Justice smile through the darkness, too, at so safe a sound.

Mrs. Douglass had Justice close, with one hand on the scruff of her neck. Playful. A bunch of them had something to say right at the same time.

"What er you doing, Dad, pickin' tomatoes in the dark of night?" Justice saying to her dad.

"Ticey, baby, did you go and chop off your hair?" Mrs. Douglass asking Justice. "It sure feels like you took a dull knife and whacked it off. What d'you go and do it for?"

"Why are you asking what I'm doing when you already seem to have figured out what I'm doing?" Mr. Douglass saying right back to Justice. "Beside which, that glare from the bloodred tomatoes prit near put my eyes out this very same day. Now, they don't dare do that in the dark."

"I didn't chop it off with a knife," Justice saying back to her mom, "I took some scissors. Never can get so many tangles of hair out in the morning."

"It looked real nice all day long," Dorian saying about her hair.

Finished, straightening up from his night work, Mr. Douglass bumped Mrs. Douglass, who stepped on Justice pretty hard; laughed when her daughter screamed like the dickens. "Oh, Tice, I'm so sorry!" She turned Justice loose.

Justice tripped into Levi. No, it was Thomas, she could tell. Had to be Thomas, like a fence-post planted in the dark. He resisted. Rather than give her a hand to guide her, the way Levi would have, Thomas pushed her roughly away. She fell into Dorian, grabbed for his neck to get some balance and they both tumbled over. A hand touched them to help them. Levi. Had to be. Justice squealed and giggled, scrambling up. Dorian giggled high just like she did.

"I think somebody fell over," Mrs. Douglass saying.

"Have 'em be careful," Mr. Douglass saying. "Holes happen to folks in a night garden. Fall into a night-garden hole is tragic. And never find your way out lest you happen by way of East Asia."

"That's a big fib, Dad," Justice saying.

"B-b-bump into *mmme* l-like th-that!" It was Thomas. Sullen, stuttering; suddenly he was angry at her.

"She didn't hurt you—how could she of hurt you?" Levi had said.

"L-like nnnothing tttouching m-m-me in-in theee d-dark."

"Oh, Thomas," Mrs. Douglass sighing.

"Ssure, t-t-take her ssside. Al-always d-do."

On and on. Them in the night-dark, half joking, most of the time having a lot of fun. The only anger coming out of Thomas when he was sure someone had slighted him in favor of his sister. Still, it was mostly a close and warm feeling they all had. Even maybe Thomas felt it for a moment or two at a time, when he let himself. It had been night and warm and mysterious. Close together, and night, and mystery. It was home and night, loving and caring.

And gone. Most likely forever.

That was all, then. The mutual feeling between Justice and Dorian pulled away from their center and back into the future. They opened their eyes. They were in Dustland. It was real. Dustland had happened to them, never to reverse and never to have been.

Justice shivered, shaking off the sadness. She felt cool, suddenly, over her body. They had passed through Dustland's unbelievable dawn an hour ago. Now what passed for day blistered with heat, without moisture. She felt excitement; felt as if she were holding herself in. Warned herself not to think deeply or risk having the land's contradictions shatter her senses.

Was the whole future a dustland, or was Dustland but a hundred, a thousand miles?

Justice turned her second sight upward again through shrouds of grit, as she had done before. Again, searching outward, her mind went beyond horizons as far as she could project it. She had no idea how far that might be. She suspected that, without the whole unit, she had not projected terribly far. She measured lumens of light. She related these to time and to space. The very continuum of it was clogged with dust. Dust curved.

"Oh, my!" Justice gasped out loud.

Above the dust she found the sky as it was at home. And the sun. And sensed that the sun was as it had always been.

Thank goodness. Then how much time would have passed?

Something else.

Her extrasensory homed in on echoes. Whispers.

What?

Thoughts floating far above the land. They were connected to no mind. They were lost, projected outward toward something called—*Star*!

There were other thoughts, she discovered. Somewhere about her and Dorian and Levi. And about someone, the prey—*Thomas*!

Justice knew whose thoughts they were.

Miacis has a god.

The pleas of Miacis were neither accepted nor

turned down by this god. For at no time in the past or in the future was the sun a thinking entity.

"How sad for Miacis," Justice said to herself. She thought about answering the pleas, about becoming Star.

Miacis must be awfully alone to try to connect with something so far away. Something she can't even . . .

A question jolted her.

How can Miacis know the sun is there, let alone that it's a star? She can't even see! If she weren't blind, what about all the dust—to know the sun's name and to call it exactly! But she does have telepathy, Justice thought. Maybe she's not aware how she came to know the sun. But knowing, the way you do by the time you can understand things. Miacis. She's so alone.

The one thing Justice had learned about Dustland was that all in it were parts of a unit or group for the sake of survival. Except for Miacis.

Justice was staring down at the dust. She had been thinking very deeply; and now scooped up handfuls of it, as a child will play with sand at the beach. Grainy and gritty, the dust slipped through her fingers. It appeared to flow.

Sure looks like dust. But it doesn't *feel* like any dust I know of, she thought.

Smaller particles rose like steam around the flow through her fingers, cohering in a mass. She thought she felt a warmth when she held the handfuls absolutely still in her palms.

Dorian watched her, looking puzzled as she gathered armfuls to her, then let the dust go. It clung to the air before it poured slowly down to the ground. He didn't take his eyes from her as she smoothed dust over her legs and feet until she was covered with it to the waist.

Steadying her will in a concentration of force. Stilled her thumping heart to a whirring. All of her senses listened and felt. Her mind penetrated.

Justice knew as much science as any bright eleven-year-old. Her second sight did not make her a scientific marvel. It acted as a truth-bearing light. But first she had to see.

*I am the Watcher.* Her mind flared in a brilliance of observing.

Dust. Motion of pulsing. Dust. A rhythm unto itself. High above, where it curved on itself and on the earth, it was the same. Pulsing, as if about to do something. To change.

She kicked the dust away, thinking: All those pieces of worlmas!

The dust slid away from her. It rose slightly around her, momentarily choking her.

What if all the pieces were still alive!

Swiftly, Justice got up and brushed dust from her hands and clothing. But it was no use. Dust was everywhere. It swirled in dust-devils on mysterious currents of air, while she felt not a breath. She would have to sit down in the dust again. And she did, as lightly as she could so as not to disturb it.

Worrying about plain old dust. Shoot!

And felt more confident.

There could be forces in Dustland waiting to alter her power, forces she couldn't yet fathom. But in the unit, hers was the balance of power.

I am the Watcher.

And steady inside her was that searching light of her knowing. It illuminated what she saw, always.

# 5

Everything about the future had brought difficulty to Levi. The grimy air was bad for him. And he seemed not to respond well to the process of time in Dustland. Time took longer in the future. Waiting, sitting, seemed prolonged. The chase of Miacis to capture Thomas was taking so much more time than it should have. Justice sensed that time was stretched, extended and slowed.

Maybe Levi is bothered so much because all of himself that was needed didn't make the Crossover to here, she thought.

She recalled Levi saying once, "I won't live long. I'm glad."

She would never forgive herself if something so unthinkable happened. But she knew it was Thomas who caused Levi the most suffering.

Giving Levi awful sights to see by magic and making him sick with it. For years!

But that was in the past. Now Thomas insisted he hadn't bothered his brother with magic since they had become the unit and time-traveled to the future.

"I hate coming here," Thomas had told her darkly. "But I wouldn't hurt him over it." And he had sworn he wouldn't harm Levi ever again.

She had believed him.

He knows we have to get Levi home, she thought. And knows none of us can return unless we're the unit. So it's a battle of wits and nerves!

Justice moved around so that she could better watch Levi. His lips had turned a greenish color. Lack of oxygen might've affected Thomas' mind as well, causing him to run out into the emptiness of Dustland.

Levi was lying on his back with his eyes closed. He seemed relaxed. But had his skin turned gray, or was the washed-out color caused by the dust covering everything?

"What skin?" Justice thought, and swiftly willed herself away from the question.

Suddenly a related one: When I'm back home, is Dustland here?

Justice, scratching at her arm, looked down, seeing her arm and hand. They were there. She saw them. And knew they couldn't be there.

The unit can be injured. Can it? Can any of us be killed?

She recalled Miacis' attack when they first encountered the animal.

I didn't use anything on her, Justice thought, still she went right through me and the others. Had Thomas become strong enough to cause them to melt away when Miacis hit them?

I doubt that. What am I doing? We're not even here! I mean, it just looks like we're here. We're here but not completely here. Oh, it'll drive me crazy if I don't stop thinking about it.

"Accept what you see, for now," she told herself. "But keep a good watch and be on your guard."

Her final pep-talk before finding something else to concentrate on.

Four ordinary worlma creatures were wriggling along in the dust together. They looked like human fingers stripped of the nails. From a distance, they had tiny faces that looked pleasant. Up close, the faces were small indentations. It was all true. Of the four, one was a dry husk. It moved and looked exactly the same as the others.

She shivered, keeping her eyes on them. She felt warm and cold at the same time. With no direct sunlight ever, what passed for Dustland day was bewilderingly hot. She and the others felt wringing wet most of the time, and bothered by thirst. Gritty dust seeped into their clothing and stuck to their skin.

What skin?

Levi had string-like lesions that spread over his neck and face. Justice had watched them form and disappear, then form again the whole time he'd been sleeping. There were worlmas near him, but Justice wouldn't let them touch him.

Thomas is dead right about this place, she thought. It's all wrong. Nothing makes any sense.

With a sharply focused flick of her thinking, she removed worlmas close to Levi. And floated them out over the dust, until the area around the cliff and pool was clear of them. In a quiver, like fingers a-tremble, they burrowed under the dust and disappeared.

Justice brushed Levi's thoughts, very lightly, so as not to disturb him.

*Try to get used to things*, gently she traced in his sleep. *Hold on. I'm sure nothing will harm you.* She felt a coolness from him, so empty.

*I never meant to get you hurt, Levi. You know I'm sorry that Thomas ran off. How could you know, you've been out all this time! Oh, I'm to blame for everything. But we mustn't stop coming here.*

Levi was still within.

She was so grateful to have him and Dorian with her. Both had agreed to become part of the unit so that all of them might enter the future. Unlike Thomas, they never fought against her.

She stared at Levi, marveling at his clothing. The bright woven tunic he wore had dyes that changed color tones. Although muted in Dustland's dull light, the colors wavered and changed hues.

When the unit entered the Crossover between times, it at some point encountered a severe turbulence. The unit hurtled through it and into the future without a stitch of clothing. Thomas saved them embarrassment by fabricating the clothes they wore. He invented wardrobes and modified them to fit the conditions of Dustland, and to suit his own whim. Yet in Dustland their made-up clothing took on real qualities. The hooded garments kept the dust off them and saved their skin from chafing with the grit.

Justice reached down and touched her brown sandals. They didn't feel exactly like the material of shoes at home in the past. But her hand didn't go straight through them as they should have with an illusion.

The feel of them might be an illusion, too, she thought. But she wasn't sure. Not yet.

When the four of them returned to the present, each had on his or her proper clothing. Thomas' magic clothing would no longer be. They'd spent hours at their favorite spot along the Quinella River trying to understand it all. Thomas seemed as confused as the rest of them; yet he might have been keeping from them something he'd discovered.

Now in Dustland the ankle-length robe Justice wore was a woven beige material, very soft and comfortable. A hood fastened beneath the collar. But the robe didn't sparkle and change colors as did the tunics the boys wore. However, their trousers were the same material as her robe.

Thomas had given himself thick-soled running shoes. Made of a stretch nylon, they would massage away soreness over a long run.

She had noticed his shoes were different from the sandals the rest of them wore, but had sensed nothing wrong. Thomas' usual hostile swagger had fooled her into thinking everything was all right.

I never thought about the shoes being really real in the first place, she thought. But the shoes are as real as this robe I'm wearing, I guess.

Her mind commenced slipping from her again. She felt slightly sick to her stomach. Tried for something solid to hold on to.

Levi. He was slimmer in the tunic. Carefully, Justice entered his mind, touching lightly and not probing at all. She met the cool emptiness in which swirled senseless fragments. She summoned Dorian. And together, very lightly, they scanned the sense and substance of Levi's inner space. Sounds of his mind were harsh.

*Do you think Thomas tearing away out of the unit did this?* Justice traced to Dorian.

*Maybe that, with the Crossover*, he traced back. They both sensed segments of more than one time.

Justice took hold. *Levi. Let yourself go. Don't think about anything. Relax.*

*I. Where . . . who? Thomas. Get.*

*Levi, Thomas ran off*, she traced. *But don't you worry about a thing. Miacis is after him and will bring him back. Then we can go home!*

She and Dorian formed a wedge of energy and forced time segments back into their proper moments.

*Don't try to talk*, Justice traced. *Don't move. Don't look around. Keep your eyes closed. It's Dustland.*

The cool emptiness did not clear. It worried Justice.

"It's the Crossover, more than anything else," Dorian told her. They released their telepathy and combined sensory from Levi and from one another. Wearily, Justice dropped her head on her arms.

Thoughts closing in on her. Miacis saying, "Why, yes, Master, there are cities in Dustland." Miacis too eager to please. Then she'd asked Justice the meaning of the word *city*. And later admitted there were no cities in Dustland. She'd become charmed by the sound of the word.

Will I know when Miacis is lying to me? Not when she doesn't know.

Her mind retreated from her. I can't fetch Thomas back, she thought. I've tried, but I can't will him by blanketing him with my sensory. Now he's too far away.

To keep following Thomas' escape, she first had to contact Miacis. Miacis might let her tap in on the trace she had on Thomas. Or maybe she wouldn't. There were times when Miacis pretended that the contact from Justice had never been made.

I don't like having her out there chasing Thomas, she thought. But she won't harm him. She's a special kind of animal. Not really alien at all.

Concerned, Dorian kept his eye on Justice. He thought to send her sensory of peace and quiet repose suggested to him by his memories of home. He missed his mother, the seer, who had uncovered the power of Thomas and Levi, as well as that of Justice. He missed the Quinella lands they all loved so much. That ancient place, with its scents of life and decay; the insects and snakes and great shade trees. These he brought visions of now to calm Justice's fears.

Justice brushed the sensory aside before it could take effect. With a blink of an eye, she denied any need of Dorian's concern.

But home. Home, she thought. Some part of us is under the buckeye tree at home. Our hands still joined back there. They have to be joined, have to stay joined, for us to make the Crossover. What do we look like there, with part of us here? When Thomas ran away here, did he let go with his hands and break the joining under the tree?

Murmuring, "He never wanted to come here. And I made him. Did I do wrong?"

Suddenly, raising her voice, "But to run out there! Even if it is to get back at me! Knowing his own brother . . ."

Dorian touched her with his healer's sympathy. And drew off some of her worry. Dorian, always unkempt at home, ragged and full of energy. Comical. Here he was calmer and appeared older. Ever alert to Justice's slightest wish, he was also on guard to the outer world. His hands fidgeted at his collar, pulling the hood over his head.

Justice watched him and softly laughed. "You're already hidden, Healer," she told him. "Thomas saw to that with the cliff. Or do you want to have magic within magic?"

He shook his head at her, raising a thumb to his lips. He traced, *Best to keep thoughts quiet now. Some one of* them *is coming.*

Justice sucked in her breath, holding herself tightly in. Someone nearly out of sight of her awareness. She had been so deep, traveling in her mind, she had missed the whole thing. Someone. Coming closer.

*Human!* A vivid second sight: *On our trail?* she traced. Her tracing trembled at the thought that someone had been trailing the unit.

*It's the same one since yesterday*, Dorian traced back. *The Terrij of the Slakers.*

*Since when? The . . . what? Why wasn't I made aware?*

She sensed Dorian's growing uneasiness. She, who held the Watcher—why would he or anyone need to make her aware?

She sensed it when Dorian arranged shields around his thinking, to save her embarrassment.

*Dorian,* calmly she traced, *if my power is less, we'll have to live with it.*

He let the shields evaporate. He knew she could penetrate them at will—could she still?

Justice had had no idea that anything was tracking them. But the possibility that her gifts were altered in the future served to calm her. Swiftly her mind toughened of itself. She grew sharply more alert.

"I flat out missed it," she told Dorian. "It won't happen again."

He hissed thinly at her through his teeth. *Speak through the mind.* Warning her: *Mom al-*

*ways did say the best thing about you was how you almost never missed the details.*

*That's it,* she traced. *I've had so much to think about, to worry from, I let myself get too much within.*

She let herself loose then. Knowledge of the being of Dustland filtered through her exceptional mind, as from the air.

Terrij. Much like a scout. A Terrij of the Slakers. A Jam people. Justice sought meaning behind these strange words. The Watcher came into her insight, lighting her eyes. Time ebbing and flowing on a tide of people. Justice knew the Slakers:

Closed in on *kelms* of hunting parties. Like all creatures of Dustland, they slept covered with dust. But they lived in the open in kelms of fifty or sixty. They bedded in groups, wrapped in one another's wings. When danger threatened, groups came to the rescue by signal from a threatened kelm. Signals were carried from one kelm to the next.

They were hunters. But not always. They were killers. In the past they had been solely scavengers, living off the kill of others. Massing near a kill, they would signal until a neighboring kelm had come in contact. They called out even when the food was barely enough to feed one kelm. An ugly fight for food would take place between the

kelms. Many would die. It took centuries for sur-
viving Slakers to think of using food for themselves.

Justice watched the vision with growing revulsion. Slakers began eating while a kill still
bled. They lapped the blood until the tissue was
dry as toast, much as Miacis did. But as soon as
a prey bled, they began eating it, nibbling away.

The Watcher observed: Place no blame.

From the beginning, Slakers were desperate
for water. They massed at kills because of the need
for moisture.

Again and again the vision showed that at first
no Slaker would kill. But the instinct for peace
went awry with the passage of time. It came to one
of them, and then to more of them, that they could
slow a prey down. They could move in; and there
were enough of them to exhaust it by keeping it
moving until it was too tired to defend itself.

Who could say when a Slaker had started tor-
menting a creature for the first time?

Justice couldn't find that point in time. It
hadn't been there in the purpose of Slakers. Then
it had been given to them.

She erased the thought at once. She watched
the vision.

Slakers discovered that hard blows could maim
a creature, crippling it so it could not move swiftly.
The next step came on the heels of the first. Killing

prey came to them easily. Slakers might scavenge or they might kill. There was no direct cause for their behavior one way or the other. They did what they did when they felt like doing it.

Not so nice, Justice thought. She revealed all she had learned to Dorian. He drew the hood tighter about his face.

*You want to see for yourself?* she traced to him.

*No.*

*I think you should,* she traced.

*Are you telling me to?*

*I think I must be,* she traced.

*Why don't you just say you're commanding me the way you command Miacis?*

*I'm not commanding you. Why are you angry all of a sudden?*

*I'm not angry,* he traced. *I just don't want to see.*

*You've never not wanted to see before. Dorian, what's wrong?*

*Nothing's wrong. I don't like this place. Justice, I'm . . . I'm afraid something's going to happen.*

*To me?* When he didn't answer, she smiled. *Don't worry, Healer. Something's going to happen, all right, but I don't think it'll hurt me. At least . . .* But she broke off. The Slaker vision would not wait. It overwhelmed other thoughts. Dorian couldn't help seeing.

*Premonition!* traced Justice.

Scattered in groups, Slakers knew by premonition of kills, of preys, of strangers near. Knowledge came to a few individuals scattered across the dustscape. And these had foreknowledge of events, apparently through the skin, with no sighted use of the mind.

A special individual of a kelm would shudder. It would communicate with another special one by impulses from its skin. The other special one would be in its own kelm and would shudder as the signal hit it. In this way, kelms would come together at a precise, foreknown place.

*Really strange!* Justice traced to Dorian.

Slakers had five extremities—two arms and three legs. The third leg was positioned at the rear of the body. It was a powerful and flexible appendage, used to fling the Slaker off the ground in an extremely high lift.

The female Slakers above the age of twelve were able to fly. Their arms were forelimbs of paired organs. They had lifting surfaces formed of membranous skin connecting the long, modified digits of their hands.

The male Slakers could not or would not fly, although they had forelimbs identical to, if not stronger than, the forelimbs of the females. They didn't use the third limb or leg in the same way as the females, for lift-off. The male third leg was a vicious weapon, used for whacking or kicking a prey. The weapon was unleashed like a fist, with the force of a half-ton weight.

*Pretty awful dudes*, traced Justice.

*Yeah, and I'm not sure the women are much better, either*, traced Dorian.

Male Slakers also used the third leg as a place to sit, to rest on, during a long search for food. Females used it this way occasionally. For the males, the membranous skin, unused for flight, served as pouches to store what was left of blood and meat from a kill after they themselves had eaten their fill. They shared the leftover food with the females. They disliked sharing, and they shared only after threats from the females. Sometime in the distant future, males more than likely would not share. Females would then die out; and so, too, the species.

*Maybe the females who learned to fly could learn to do more than threaten. Why don't they try something else?* Justice traced, unsure of what she meant by that.

There was no reply from Dorian.

Now they could see the Slaker, the Terrij, who had followed them. It came toward them from the far side of Thomas' cliff. It came up from behind them. In their sighted way, they could see it come warily on.

The creature had to feel their presence; yet it

was clear that it couldn't actually see them. It perceived Thomas' cliff with the fallen rocks and showed a disturbance akin to astonishment. It slowed down, then stopped completely. After a paralyzed pause, in which its breathing was a continuous, churning groan, it came cautiously forward.

The Slaker moved in an uncertain pattern, with the oddest rhythm Justice had ever seen. It leaned back on its third leg. Without appearing to have moved, it was instantly in a place forward from where it had just been. An incredible change of place.

I missed something, Justice thought.

But as the Terrij came on, Justice knew that the sequence, the movement itself, had been left out. The Terrij would be in one place, lean on the leg and would be closer.

It had come this way before, but had never encountered a cliff. Staring at the rock, its eyes were glittering wild. It moved its legs as if climbing. It raised winged arms to grab hold of the rocks. Its robe fell open. Justice saw that the Terrij was a female; sensed that she would change in the last stage of maturity.

Nambnua was one of her names. Meaning *wifeman stalker*. The Terrij was best called Bambnua—Dustwalker—which was both a title and a name.

Suddenly, everything happened too fast, in flashes before Justice's and Dorian's unaccustomed eyes.

The Bambnua moved in incredible bursts of being in one place, then in another. She discovered the water pool. She beat her chest, flapping her wings. She drank deeply from the pool. Her skin broke out in welts as she began signaling her kelm.

She was back at the cliff, trying to climb, and did not uncover Justice and Dorian. Yet she knew something, felt something there. She whirled around and around, trying to find them. She found Levi. She could have been a statue standing there, she was that still. Not a muscle moved for at least ten minutes. They watched her, not daring to think. Without any warning, she was at Levi's side. A rush of air from her mouth seemed to slide down the dust. It fell in whispers around her feet. Sounds and breaks, language, unlike anything they had ever heard.

The Terrij, Bambnua, reached for Levi with the finger-like digits at the end of winged forearms before Justice could think what to do. The hands, the winged arms went right through him.

Time hung over them in the dust. Justice and Dorian were stunned. Before their eyes, the form of Levi vanished. And the Terrij hawked a keening sound.

# 6

_____

Toward the middle of Nolight the two of them began making their way once again. Their extra-sensory allowed them to see with little more effort than was needed in daylight. Thomas kept himself loose as he jogged through the wasteland. He calculated that they were running in twenty-minute bursts, which they alternated with brisk walks of a half-hour or so. Only one of them at any one time was conscious of the power of endurance, of a shortness of breath or fatigue. Whenever Thomas got tired, he would release his brother Levi's senses, now carried in the back of his mind. Levi would then become the aware one. And still walking or jogging beside Levi, Thomas would rest his own senses inside Levi's head.

This cooperation between them worked well to ease Thomas' desperate need to put as much space between himself and Miacis as he could for as long as he could. Yet, from the moment he had run, he had known that Miacis would chase him and eventually would catch him. It was all part of his plan.

The Nolight of Dustland grew monotonous. Thomas imagined he was alone, tricked by his senses into thinking he was on a treadmill which carried him through unending time. His fear grew unbearable that Miacis would overtake him before he was ready.

The next moment Thomas remembered how cleanly he had stolen Levi from under Justice's powerful protection. His breaking from the unit had knocked each of them senseless. He had been ready for that and quickly come to. He'd taken over his brother's unconscious mind and left Levi's illusion.

Now Thomas ran through Dustland with Levi at his side. However, they could not possibly be running. But they were. He was definitely running, definitely escaping. He knew he was on his way, but maybe he was headed nowhere, to no purpose.

Abruptly, Thomas came to, hearing Levi call him from in back of his own mind. Thomas had fallen asleep on his feet again, as he would do when he was at the edge of exhaustion. He found himself standing still in the Nolight with a mindless Levi at his side.

*Yeah?* answering Levi's call. *How long have I been out? Were you asleep, too?*

Levi traced from the back of Thomas' mind: *I must've been asleep. But I don't think either of us was out for long. I usually wake up fast when you stop in your tracks like that.*

*Yeah.* Through his thoughts Thomas caught the strain Levi was under. He had no time to dwell on it, however. For Dustland's striking dawn was upon them.

He traced a quick warning: *Brace yourself!*

The persona of Levi cringed and lay low in back of Thomas' mind.

Thomas never permitted himself to admit how truly spectacular was Dustland's dawning. He held fast to his hate of all aspects of the future. He told himself that, here, dawn was a sideshow lit up in a carnival. He stuck out his chin and chest, with his hands firmly on the bone weapons around his waist. He wasn't going to wince. And made faces, stuck out his tongue, as the dawn grew. He would show his weakling brother, safe in his own head, that nothing in the world at any time could scare *him.*

Light of dawn broke and splintered. It attached to every particle of dust. In the air and on the ground, waves of dust grew miraculous with lights. Thomas breathed in and exhaled colors. His clothing was coated with rainbows. The space around him danced with a dizzying array of multicolored sparks.

I can hold blues in the palms of my hands!

He mixed greens with orange on his tongue. A simple flexing of arm muscles sent colors caroming at a thousand angles. Bloodred eddies and golden flurries skidded against mauve caps of dust breaking against his chest and shoulders.

He could feel the Levi persona quiver in awe.

*Baloney!* Thomas traced. He could close his eyes and tone down the colors, but never could he quite shut them out.

A choked tracing: *Tom-Tom, seeing is believing.*

*Baloney, man!* Stubbornly, Thomas fought to keep his fury.

In no time the light show of colors began fading, probably when the sun rose above the horizon. The dust felt warm, heating up uncomfortably.

*Go ahead and believe whatever you want*, he suddenly traced to Levi. *It's the way it is, just like we saw it.*

He stared grimly at the light fixed to dust as it thinned and fell in shards. These dimmed and vanished, leaving the dry heat. Dustland brought forth its dismal, murky day.

It was Levi's turn to carry them; that is, to feel and think for both of them. Thomas' persona would now rest in his mind. And Levi came out and back into his own self—what *could* you call that part of them that seemed to walk, move, have bodies in Dustland? Thomas' persona flowed into his. Yet Levi did not have his brother's endurance. All he could manage was a painful stiff-legged trudge through the dust.

*We can rest here, if you want to,* Thomas traced. *Lee, you want to rest here?*

*Here is any different from back there or up ahead?*

"I was only thinking of you," Thomas said. He found that, within Levi's mind, there was no need for him to trace.

*Well, you don't have to think of me. The sooner we get farther, the farther away we'll be.*

"That makes a lot of sense," Thomas said.

*Makes as much sense as thinking it matters whether I rest,* Lee traced wearily.

"I'm just trying to help you."

*Since when have you thought about me, Tom-Tom? Why you forced me out on this—this death run . . . I know it wasn't to help* me.

They were silent. Levi stumbled, fell to one knee. He got up, brushing himself off.

"You do need to stop. You can't go on much longer."

*If I stop, I won't get going again and Miacis will catch you—is that what you want to happen?*

"I thought you were on *their* side."

*I'm not on anybody's side.*

"But you go along with Her Majesty, with letting Justice lead us into this stink-hole over and over again."

*It has nothing to do with going along with her,* Levi traced. *It's . . . it's that I know she is the Power.*

"Wouldn't be too sure of it if I was you. Least, not here."

*She is the Power, Tom-Tom. And if she believes we have to come here, that it's her place, her destiny, I guess you call it, to be here—well, then I'll do my part to help her get here.*

"Even when it means half-killing yourself," Thomas said.

A pause. They both were aware of the draining effect Dustland seemed to have on Levi.

*Even that,* finally Levi traced.

"Well, you must need to suffer, buddy. I always knew you had some love of misery. Some death wish!"

*Couldn't be worse than living with you always torturing me.*

Thomas couldn't think of a reply. He remembered he had promised his dumb sister, *blind* Justice, that he would never again use his power on his brother. Of course, he'd lied. What did she expect, the truth?

And now he felt smothered in Levi's sorrowing mind. He needed to break out, and he did so. Found himself walking along a few paces in front of Lee. And felt like turning, snarling back at his dummy brother. But what good was it going to do? He shrugged and headed on.

When they walked with each other this way, with neither of them within the other's mind, Thomas made them both invisible. Nothing whatever of them showed. Although their mind-tracing and talking was as sharp and alive as ever, their physical condition was awful to see, and the reason Thomas kept them invisible. He had blisters on his lips from the daytime grinding heat. His mouth hurt, too. Both his eyes and Levi's were red- . rimmed and strained. Lee had lesions on his neck; festering liquid seeped from them, running in stringy rivulets down his chest.

Thomas wouldn't let himself think about what was possible, and what was real and not real. Blisters, lesions, dust all over them—what was *them*? How was it they carried each other's persona? How to walk or run, the same as they did at home? He knew his skeleton was within his body. But his good sense told him that neither his skeleton nor his body could be here in the future. That went for Levi and the rest of them. Hard enough understanding that their minds were here.

He shivered at the thought of his mind trapped in Dustland and his real, solid and alive body off in the past. Home. A yearning for home touched him deeply and caused him to strangle a cry.

But if the body is at home, what is this, blistering and hurting? Stumbling from exhaustion?

His mind shifting. To die in Dustland? was his next thought. For us, maybe just a feeling of death.

He opened the mysterious corridor between his mind and Levi's. It was a one-way conduit from him, through which his brain waves flowed and summoned the identical brain waves of his brother. They fused as one. The passageway allowed Thomas to connect telepathically with Levi whenever he felt like it and to break the connection at will. Levi could not trace telepathically without Thomas or one of the others to start.

Thomas repeated what he had been thinking, adding, *If there's no body to die, how does the mind know to stop?*

*Then it can't,* Levi traced, not a bit surprised by the intrusion of Thomas' morbid speculation. For he had become obsessed with similar thoughts. *In Dustland we can't die. Only if something hurt us back home. If our for-real bodies got battered— I mean, our arms and heads and stuff—and our lives came to an end. Would all of us here, whatever there is of us here, go . . . poof?*

*That's what I think,* Thomas traced. *That's how I think it would have to be. That's the reason I make it so we can't see ourselves right now. Because, seeing us out here with no food for who knows how long it has been, well, logic has to tell us we're hurting and losing strength.*

*But in the mind, mind-tracing, we're as strong as ever!*

*You got it,* Thomas traced quietly.

*So here we have to be only—mind.*

*Mind it is and mind it has always been,* traced Thomas. *Mind your P's and Q's,* he joked.

*But, Tom-Tom, when you're not making us invisible, we can see . . .*

Abruptly, Thomas closed the corridor between them. He erased the sentence fragment as Lee formed it. At once he made them visible so Lee would have something else to occupy him other than what Thomas believed was a dangerous line of thought. Like Justice, he was beginning to uncover a clue to the mystery of Dustland.

They, all of them, were *mind*-travelers in Dustland. *They* knew that.

Levi shuddered at the sight of his own self. He had always distrusted his body, which grew weaker and more sickly with each time-travel. And now he hollered out as he glimpsed his bloody feet. The grinding quality of the dust had worn away his socks through his sandals. Seeing the wounds, he felt the pain. And moaned softly, done in at last.

Thomas knew he had to get him holed up somewhere right away. And this was as far as his plans would take Levi.

*There's some shelter up ahead. Lee? I think I see some rocks. You can rest by them.*

*Where . . . where are they?*

*Right up ahead. There!*

Rocks worn smooth and shining dully through the gloom, as if dimly illuminated from within.

Thomas couldn't help smiling to himself. He could create the images he needed here in Dustland the same as he could at home. Here his magic was even better. It felt larger and more real than anything he imaged at home. He couldn't be sure how good he was; he just got better and better.

The rocks up ahead were as real as any clump Thomas had seen anywhere. And yet he wasn't certain if he had built them there by thinking he needed them, or if he'd suddenly really seen them through the murk where they'd always been.

Well, does it matter? he asked himself. He was becoming at ease with Dustland's eerie qualities.

I'm not going to let this place spook me the way it has Justice. Getting into what is and isn't so real will turn you clear around. If she keeps at it, she'll never work her way out. Which suits me just fine! But definitely the word here is *weird*. Something sure is going down. Not so sweet, either.

He was sure something strange was going on. And he surrounded the thought in a thick and searing cold, a subterranean gloom of icewalls that nothing could penetrate.

Mind shifting again, thinking: Oh, man. What is and what isn't! But I have to admit, it's the most exciting, oddest thing I've ever been into. If I can find out how it all works, I bet I could . . . take over! Wouldn't *that* be something? But never let Justice know. Don't look at things too closely yourself. It messes up your mind if you do. Don't dare.

The rocks loomed. Dust hanging in shrouds which curled and waved slowly across the windless land. Dust thicker than ever.

Levi commenced coughing. By the time they had reached the rocks, he was gasping for air. He leaned close to Thomas for protection.

Thomas tasted grit. He wrapped his arms around his brother's head and neck, covering him as best he could.

*Try breathing through the hood of your tunic like I'm doing*, Thomas traced. *Here, pull it up and around . . .*

*What hood?* gasping, Levi traced. *You made up these clothes!*

*Look, there's something real about everything I make up here. You know there is. And wouldn't it be—* He broke off and started over. *We'll figure it out later. Now, just do what I tell you.*

Bowed down against the rocks, Levi held the hood to his mouth. It did seem to help. The dust had gotten so thick he had to keep his eyes shut tight.

*Good thing we don't have to open our mouths to talk*, Thomas traced.

Levi broke in on him, etching thoughts in slivers: *You'll get through. I bet if anyone can survive this, it'll be you.*

*Stop being so dumb.* Holding himself in against feeling.

*Tom-Tom? We aren't here, are we? You said our bodies weren't.*

Echoes in Thomas' brain like gusts of wind. Sounds of Levi struggling to breathe. Wind sounds in a backward-and-forward flow, as if from the past, where their bodies waited, to the future.

*Better not think*, Thomas traced.

Lee's dread spread out around them. He whined: *Tom-Tom? My feet. Can't you do something?* Through caked dust, Levi's feet oozed blood.

*Think I'm some healer?* Thomas stormed. *Well, I'm not.* Irritated into being reminded of Justice, and Dorian, the healer.

Wouldn't mind having Dorian along, though, Thomas thought.

The illusion of Lee he'd made for them had to be still working. Justice would think her favorite brother was still safe beside her. And Miacis would think so, too. If all went as Thomas planned, it would be the real Levi that Miacis brought back and not himself. Thomas grinned. He could hear Justice now, chewing out the dog.

He sniffed the choking dust.

Miacis!

Ever alert, Thomas cut through the dust with his clairvoyance, sensing back along their trail. He used his finely tuned power with caution, fully expecting the animal to still be on their course but at a distance from them. It wasn't long before he homed in on a life-form racing through.

What shocked him was how close the beast had come. He could sense the sweat-drenched fur, muscles rippling and surging beneath.

Tricked me! How'd she—? Must've missed a sense-post. Man!

Miacis was closing in. He had to get away at once.

Thomas had planned ahead, however. Not far behind, he had set up an illusion to slow Miacis down. He'd erected a mighty scaffolding in her way. It was packed with quivering shapes clinging to the supports and braces. Thomas had crash-landed their space vehicle some distance from the scaffolding. Gradually he had expanded the scaffolding into a slime-coated grandstand.

Wait till she hits that baby—it's sweet!

For it was one of his finest illusions. There were twisted forms, perhaps human, lying quite still in the dust surrounding the crash site. The whole scene was planted to strike terror in anyone stumbling upon it. Those who had survived the entry into earth-future sat up in the arena, shrouded in a mildewing silence.

*She's close. Close! She's in!*

Thomas homed in telepathically as Miacis entered the illusion.

She would be his prey. If he could just terrify the wits out of her, she would turn tail and run. And she would become *his* slave.

*Something's wrong!*

Miacis wasn't slowing down. She wasn't seeing anything.

Thomas closed his eyes and saw.

*So that's it!* It hit him that Miacis simply couldn't see a single thing. An illusion had to be seen before it could work.

*Stone blind as a bloody bat! I let her catch up and she can't even see! Well, she won't catch* me!

Miacis would catch Levi. Thomas would place his own aura around his brother, enclosing Levi in the atmosphere of his being. The aura of mental and physical imprints intertwined were similar to scents. Never could they be mistaken for the imprints of anyone else once they were in place.

*What of Lee's aura?*

It was not very strong, almost never over-powering. Thomas would thin it out, expand it as far as was safe.

Not to destroy it. Just to put his own in place over it, so you wouldn't know it was there.

Discovering Thomas' aura, Miacis wouldn't question that the boy she captured was anyone but Thomas.

And then Thomas would blank out Lee's brain and fill it with a fake persona. He would leave clues of himself in Lee's thin blood and weak muscle.

Just in case Miacis should decide to check it all out, he thought.

*Miacis!*

Legs churning in a frenzy of running. Her coat as shiny as metal, the grinding dust polishing every hair. Miacis ranging. Tracking. Never tiring. Nothing in Dustland a hindrance to her.

Like searing steam on Thomas' mind was Miacis' good humor on his backtrail.

Have to get away from here!

*Tom-Tom?* It was Lee.

*Yeah?* as calmly as he could trace it.

Lee's eyes were shut tight. *Tom-Tom.* He clutched at the rocks. *I'm breathing through the dust, through my hood, like you told me.*

*Yeah. That's good.*

*But you know I can't breathe through anything.*

*Because I don't have anything here to breathe with.
My flesh and bone isn't here—right? So what is it
I hear and feel breathing? What walked out here
and ran—is it me in the past keeps me breathing
here—? Tom-Tom? I feel like I'm in a box. I'm
afraid I'll suffocate!*

A distance grew in his desperate thoughts, as
if some part of him had snapped and separated
from the other. Suddenly he was cut off from a
sense of the familiar. He was overwhelmed with
sadness. His squeezed-shut eyes dribbled uncon-
trollable tears.

What eyes?

He never knew the moment Thomas slipped
away. But, slowly, awareness came to him and
revealed that his brother had abandoned him.

*Tom-Tom. Why did you do this?*

A largeness spread out inside Levi. Huge, it
forced its way throughout his inner space. The
fake persona squeezed Levi into a corner. It blan-
keted his mind. What remained of his senses gathered on the far side of knowing in a tiny puff of
nothing. Thomas' aura was all.

So it was that the brother waited. He clung to
rocks a few inches from the ground. In case Miacis
was already upon him, he pretended he needed
rest. Dust gathered strangely around him, howling
and blowing, streaming its way into rock crevices.
With whistling force, it made its way under the

brother's fingers. Until it covered him, caking him in a putrid grime, which gave him the form and tint of some ancient gargoyle. He who had been Levi might never have existed. Yet Levi was present in form. He represented the two who were so much the same before the form took on a certainty of character. It soon became wholly the brother Thomas.

The brother Thomas crouched, unmoving, yet fierce. He felt exactly like some deformed creature carved from the stone. However, he managed to appear bold and defiant. He had a sudden unpleasant tingling in every joint of his body. And knew Miacis would soon be nibbling at his toes.

Not thirty yards away was the one who was truly Thomas. He was hidden at the side of another clutch of rocks. He intended using his clairvoyance to know what transpired between Miacis and Levi when Miacis arrived. As self in control of Levi's mind, he had felt tingling and knew Miacis would soon be there.

There came a sharp tug on his foot. A painful nip at his left heel. Thomas leaped up and whirled around.

What—?

There was no one there. What had taken place must have happened to Levi. Over there, Miacis had greeted Levi by nipping at his heel. Over there, the brother sighed and climbed down the rocks. He spat dust from his mouth and snorted it from his nose.

Thomas, watching himself perform, had an urge to applaud himself, but knew better.

*You win, I give up*, the brother traced to Miacis. *I'm too weak to outrun you. But there'll be other times—right? So take me back, dog. I'm starving.* Spoken just the way the real Thomas would have.

Miacis' shrill laughter pierced the gloom. It broke off in a wheedling bark.

Suddenly Thomas had a striking premonition that his best-laid schemes were blown. In one moment everything he had planned would fall apart, blasted by the dust into smithereens.

# 7

---

Thomas had known storms. He'd even seen one terrible one with anvil heads seventy-thousand feet up, his dad had said. Out of that storm had come a violent twister that uprooted fifty-year-old trees before it lifted to vanish in darkest clouds.

At the age of three, he and Levi had witnessed the queerest weather of all. Sitting close together on the couch, they ate popsicles and peered out of the window. Thomas remembered how strange it had felt to be inside in a calm place when everything had gone wild outside. They watched a garbage can fly down the street. The lilac bushes bent over so far, their blooms touched the grass. All of the trees were on a terrific slant, as though they'd suddenly decided to lie down. He and Levi could hear a mournful howling outside their window. And Levi had said, Thomas recalled, that the sky did not look happy. What had seemed so extraordinary at the time was that he and Levi had seen nothing that could have caused all the bushes to bow down. And this, their first windstorm, had filled them with curiosity and had not frightened them in the least.

Thomas had witnessed these awesome forces of the earth and had not been harmed by them. Yet he certainly knew not to trust nature to be thoughtful toward humans. But nothing he could have imagined, nothing in the world, would have prepared him for the Rollers of Dustland.

Earlier, by the pool, Miacis had made confusing remarks about Rollers.

She had traced, *Not for the faint-featured, no siree, messengers. Fine sailing, though. Best of drum-rolling. Sure be, do!*

Her odd English had been accompanied by definite word-sounds from her throat.

Now the Roller came. It was not only alien, it was not even a part of any nightmare that Thomas had ever had. It was unheard of.

The Roller started under his feet. He felt a tremble and a twitching down there beneath the dust. As the trembling neared the surface, it took on sound. Spreading outward, the sound grew, as if out of his heels. It lengthened in waves in every direction. Thomas was sure it was going to be a quake when all at once the dust started swaying to and fro. His feet slipped from under him exactly as though someone had pulled a rug out. Thomas fell hard on his shoulders, hitting rocks and scraping along them.

Pain numbed him in flashes of cold. His mind seemed blank; for a moment he could not utter a sound. The dust slipping away stunned him; he realized he was sliding away with it. But the rocks had not moved.

Thomas grabbed them and held on. Without warning, his clairvoyance ceased. The connection he had with his fake persona inside Levi's head went out like a snuffed candle. He was all of himself back inside himself again.

And heard Levi cry out from the gloom: "Tom-Tooommm!" Through the swirling, seething murk, the sound was forlorn and full of fear.

"Lee? *Lee?*" Thomas yelled at the top of his lungs. Have to get over there, he thought. "Leeeee!"

He didn't want to let go of the rocks. If he could just hold on, he'd be safe, he knew he would.

"Don't let go!" he hollered over at Levi. Sputtering and coughing as dust filled his mouth. "Hold . . . hold on . . . Lee!"

A feeling rose in him, pure and sweet, like the kite he and Lee had flown in the field at home when they were ten. It was brother-love, making Thomas need to protect the weaker one of them. He heaved himself up. Against his will and good sense, he pushed away from the rocks, realizing that by now Miacis would know that the one she had nipped on heel was not Thomas. He spun around, already on his way to Levi, only to crash back for protection at the sight of what lay before him.

The dust was rising. It came up like a curtain, pulling in on itself from a wide distance around. Like a vast body of water, it surged and lifted, curling into a gigantic wave.

Roller.

It rose higher and higher, never breaking and falling as any wave would. A hundred feet up and up, as far as Thomas could sense through the stinging dust, which fast moved away from him. The ground had been cleaned to bare, hard earth. Almost all of the dust had by now been lifted into the vortex of the Roller. And so immense, so solid, like a mountain, the stupendous wave began moving.

It rolled side to side with a grating sound for at least a half-mile. Then it rolled forward and back at angles, making pulsating noises. From a distance on the left it advanced with the dust floating up within it, as snow rises and falls crazily in a paperweight.

It rolled toward Thomas. A tremendous force commenced pulling at him. Sucking at him with such power, it tore him from his hold on the rocks. And it pulled his hair straight up from his scalp.

*What hair?*

"Stop . . . stop it!" Thomas shouted. He found he was sobbing, and his breathing was clear of dust for the first time.

"Stop it? Why, certainly we'll stop it. Bender, fleer—see how I gather deep-words? How we mislike escapers. How far I learn-speak? Clear before you time, runaway. Ha! Clean before you past. I take you Justice dwelling, sucker!"

Miacis, skulking, slithering on her belly out of the enormous rolling wave. She was actually speaking in a darting, animal voice. It was husky, yet soft. She had finally learned how to do it. Her huge, empty eyes shone through the murk, glinting red in their centers. Behind her outsized ears, her breathing membranes glowed savagely.

Miacis slithered on her back. She stretched, seeming to lengthen, then curved herself forward. She stood on her hind legs to tower above Thomas. The bristle-hair of her underbelly glinted golden, like spikes of polished steel. She was eight, ten feet over him.

Miacis roared. The unearthly rumbling pierced Thomas' head and mind. He screamed in terror. Then his fear howled in defiance.

Thomas leaping for Miacis with one of the bone claws she had hewn for him clutched in his fist. He lunged for her throat, with all of the will he had in him in the bone claw's thrust.

So sudden an assault took Miacis by surprise. Thomas had dodged her forelegs and was close in on her vulnerable underside before she could move to stop him. The shock did not last long.

Thomas raked the claw across her chest, leaping up high against her to do so. The claw caught on the bristle-hair and became tangled.

Miacis whined a deadly sound. *Runaway! We mislike dust-runners. But now me have me dummy-drummer Tom-Tom!* This she traced in stinging lines across his mind. And tightened her arms around him. Soon Thomas was surrounded. He was smothered in fur.

And felt her dewclaws make tiny punctures. Something cool, dizzying, flowed under his shoulderblades.

Miacis roared and yipped.

"We have to get a move on, stop for the other one. Knew you must-a had him with you. Felt no him back there lying down beside me and Master."

Thomas was wrenched forward by the Roller's pull. Noise poured down from above. He was rising over Miacis' head. But then she began rising too, and she was soon right next to him. The two of them rose in the immense, rolling dustwave.

"Merrily, merrily," crooned Miacis.

Up and up they went. Thomas could hear the rise, although he could not now move any part of himself. He wondered, briefly, how was it she could drug him by pricking him with her claws when he had no body here. But the thought would not hold still.

Going up the Roller was like a lifting, the way sails fill and balloon. He reached the Roller's crest. There at the height Miacis pushed and tugged at him until his head poked through the top of the Roller.

I have no head. I am not! Not here!

But the sensation was real enough. The Roller held his arms up. The top of it was taut, like the skin of an umbrella. Miacis sat neatly to one side of him. She growled contentedly, licking her dew-claws.

In a moment the Roller stopped. Somehow Miacis flowed down through its dust. A short life-time of churning noise idling, and she was back, with Levi.

*Lee!*

Levi hung there, facing Thomas. His arms were spread out the same way. Thomas saw that their hands were touching, although he felt nothing. He could find no way to contact Levi's brain.

Their arms made a crooked circle. Miacis leaped into the circle. Sitting tall, she blinked brightly at them, unseeing.

Their heads lolled. Both of them tried desperately to speak. They tried to make sense out of everything. Thomas could not mind-trace, nor open the mysterious corridor between him and his brother. With each passing second, both of them grew more disoriented.

Above the pounding, grating, immense Roller, the sky was blue as far as they could see. The air was cool and crisp, like a fall day. The sun, not terribly warm in this season, shone in its normal brilliance. On a gust of wind, rusty leaves rose and fell. Thomas longed to touch them. Ached to make them crumble. There was a thin scent of . . . he could not name it . . . mind confused . . . scent of . . . smoke!

Levi, too, tried to follow the fall of leaves with his unsteady gaze. As if the leaves were the last straw, he fainted dead away.

Thomas felt himself going, too. He fought against losing his senses. Fought hard.

. . . . Nothing stands alone in Dustland. This, Thomas recalled knowing in a tangle of other thoughts:

All things are joined in Dustland. Then, why Miacis?

All went dark for Thomas.

The Roller moved and hummed and carried them on. Miacis relaxed between the boys, circled by their arms. She flicked her tail. Looked at it, sensing its golden light. Its curl, its switching and thumping, felt marvelous.

This Roller a goodly Roller, thought Miacis.

She appreciated the Roller. She did not know what force it was. Never had she questioned the phenomenon. Rollers lived as she lived, always, so she believed. They were and she was. They rose, came and went. Fell. Each time of coming, one of them carried her on high to the wonder of all, Star.

"Speak me, hold me. Touch. Warm me," murmured Miacis.

She lifted her face, her eyes open to the sun. Blind eyes now. She had no memory that they had been any other way. Never had there been a blue sky for her. She had no knowledge of blue. And yet she had an instinct for its shade; the hue of it was the depth of her sightlessness. For her, the all of all things was goodly Star.

The sun made no answer. Miacis accepted its warmth as greeting enough. Let it slide under her fur to her skin. For this time, it was all she needed. However Star might speak to her, she knew that warmth was part of the message.

The Roller thundered. Miacis sensed sparks down in it, and lightning strands of powerful frictions. She knew the dust eventually would overheat the Roller. When the dust heated hotter than the hottest turn-time of Star, it would need room for expansion. The circumference of the Roller could not expand fast enough. It would blow out in a mighty explosion. Dust bursting free in sheets. Miacis knew; she had felt them slip past her, as if pulled to the ground by magnets. Veils, sheets, patterns of dust spreading out over the land. She had never seen this. Believing was not necessarily seeing. She knew all she needed and nothing more.

"Home now. Master dwelling," she said softly in her new voice as the Roller progressed across Dustland.

The identical boys remained unconscious at the Roller's height. The golden beast watched over them. Now the Roller's peripheral force literally pulled creatures into it. Small beasties, legs churning, struggled in front of it, trying to stay out of the vortex. Large lumps of things held on to one another, hoping to gather enough power to stay free. Huge things, like bundles of cotton with brown twigs sticking out in all directions, bounced in frantic jumps ahead of the Roller. One such outlandish bundle got caught in the Roller force and came charging back. With an ear-splitting pop and snap, its legs hit the Roller and broke. There was a sickening whunk as it burst against the Roller energy and splattered in every direction.

"Stupid worlmas," Miacis muttered. She flicked and flung her ravishing tail.

The great Roller grew more huge; higher it

went, and Miacis mewed at the sun. Only the whunk and splatter of worlma-balls seemed to disturb her.

"Dumb bunnies!" she whinned. "Dead or alive, you is worthless. I'm the boss of this city!"

So Miacis was. Wherever she sensed, high up, over the vastness of the Roller of Dustland, and by the power of her nearness to Star, she was indeed top dog.

# 8

Justice sat, stricken with horror. There on the ground was the form of Levi dissolving before her eyes. And Thomas—oh, that awful Thomas!—had tricked her with make-believe so advanced it was beyond imagining.

What she had believed was Levi had been close by her and Dorian for the whole time of Thomas' escape. She had assumed he had been struck deeply by Thomas breaking free, but there had been no reason to doubt that Levi was still himself. Justice had even entered his mind. Of course, she had found that peculiar emptiness. But now she was shocked beyond belief to see him disappear.

At once she knew that Thomas had taken the real Levi with him. And, shuddering, she grieved at the thought of Levi hurt or dying in the wastes of Dustland.

What will Thomas do to him? she wondered. Why has he taken him?

She had a sinking feeling inside, realizing that Thomas' power seemed to grow with every visit the unit made to the future.

Because he uses his power so often—that's why he gets stronger?

She had cautioned Dorian and had, herself, refrained from exerting any more mind energy over things than was absolutely necessary, for fear of unknown effects. She didn't believe what they might do here could change anything in the past.

How could it change anything, when no Miacis ever existed there, or Slakers either. But am I wrong to hold back the power now, when Thomas uses his to hurt his brother?

Still stunned, she couldn't think clearly, could no longer judge. And she despaired at having let Thomas get away with Levi.

I've missed it all. I flat out missed what he was up to.

And that frightened her. Confused, she wanted to cry for help, but knew there was none here for her.

The winged humanoid stood, gaunt and shaken to see an image fade. Suddenly, in Justice's tortured mind, she became sinister, evil. That innocent creature who had stumbled into Thomas' cliff magic, only to bring the form of Levi abruptly to an end, Justice now blamed for everything.

"Get back from there!" She turned on the

Slaker, giving the Bambnua, the Dustwalker, the brunt of her fearful rage.

"You! Get *away* from him, you awful thing!" Screaming like a child at the Terrij to move away from the place in the dust where Levi's image had been.

Swiftly, Dorian telepathed soothing power to calm Justice. *Levi was never even there, you know that. The Terrij didn't have anything to do with it.*

Nothing he did could stop Justice. She sprang up. In an instant she was beside the Bambnua.

And swung at the towering being. Stiff-armed, Justice's hands clasped into a fist, all of her might was behind the swing, like side-winding an ax to fell a tree. The force of the blow shook Justice. It knocked the creature off-balance.

An absolutely alien gleam came into the Slaker's eyes.

Dimly, Justice knew she had not struck out with her hands. She had appeared to swing her arms. Yet, vaguely, she understood she had struck with her mind.

*I have no arms here. I am thought alone.*

She knew she shouldn't have struck out at a being who had done her no harm. Her good sense returned. "I didn't mean to. I'm so sorry!" choking out the words.

The Terrij staggered because of the suddenness of the attack. She had fallen to one knee to regain her balance. Now she got up again, without seeming to raise herself. Suddenly she was whirling around and around a few feet above the ground. Her unearthly wings were at half-span, but were still more than six feet across. The wings did not beat the air for the lift-up. They commenced a violent trembling. They somehow took hold of the air to shape it under the wingspread. The Terrij's third leg acted as a coiled spring, bouncing her up off the ground.

Without warning, the Bambnua was in low-grade flight. She was first in one place, then in another, with no sequence of time in between. Seeing her place and place again, merely seeing her at once so alien and so human, was terrifying. And amazing.

Justice and Dorian had moved close together without realizing it. Now they clutched each other's arms. They stared in awe at the Slaker, the Terrij, the Bambnua, Dustwalker.

*It's an angel*, Dorian traced when at last his thoughts could move again. *But I never thought an angel would be so huge.*

*It's not an it at all. Don't you remember?* traced Justice back. *She's a she. And she can't see us. That's why she lifted off, to protect herself from what she can't see.*

*Well, she saw Thomas' image of Levi.*

*Sure,* traced Justice, *and the cliff, too. She can see the magic.*

*We aren't here either, really,* traced Dorian. *But we can see ourselves, just like some illusion.*

*Well, I know,* she traced, *but our minds are real, aren't they? She can't see us, that woman being can't, but she can sure* feel *us. She knows something is here. She felt me when I hit her, bet you she did. I'm sorry for that.*

*Know you didn't mean it,* Dorian traced.

*Yeah, but she doesn't know that. She doesn't know what* hit *her.*

Justice let go of Dorian and moved a little away from him, closer to the Slaker. The Bambnua's sub-flight carried her yards away from them.

"What are you going to do?" whispered Dorian.

"Don't worry, you don't have to talk so low," Justice said calmly. "She can't hear you."

The Terrij hovered, searching the ground. Apparently, she saw and heard nothing.

I want her to know I'm waiting for her on this ground, Justice thought.

And wanted the Bambnua to comprehend that what was here that she couldn't see would not harm her or her kind. That the presence wanted only to communicate with her.

Don't know how I can get it across to her.

Deep down, Justice hoped to discover some

*1 1 1*

key to Dustland. And find some meaning for her own driving need to know the future.

I am the Watcher.

The Watcher's power was present. Justice walked toward the Dustwalker and within her was a vast quiet of watching.

Dorian knew to stay where he was unless he was summoned. He had seen the Watcher come into Justice's eyes.

And Justice waited for the Terrij to grow calm, hoping the creature would wing to the ground on her own.

But the Bambnua continued to swoop about the air in shifts of momentum. Each change in the Dustwalker's position appeared to take place in another dimension. What Justice and Dorian saw was the new location.

I am the Watcher.

She could not see any part of the Slaker's maneuver to get to the next place.

She would have to move so fast that our slower eyes would miss the motion, Justice thought.

I am the Watcher.

It came to her that the Slaker was invisible for a split second each time.

Who's to say what is the order of things here and now? Now would have to have its own order outside the physical laws we know. Perhaps they are laws that in our time were not uncovered.

I am the Watcher.

Why must this be *our* future? But if this is not *our* future, then whose is it? That creature's. Miacis'.

Convinced that this was not the unit's future. Yet it was the future of Dustland.

*A* future, but not ours.

All at once Justice felt tired.

I am the Watcher.

It held her in Its whole observing. A wave of feeling rushed from her to curl around the Terrij. Its force of caring brought the creature to the ground. The Bambnua, Dustwalker, fought hard against it. She flapped mighty wings, until the weight of the Watcher's knowing made them fall still.

The Watcher will not harm you.

Wavering motion. An enormous tremor of light and dark was the Watcher's thinking, hugely magnified. Observing.

The terrified creature did at last settle down facing Justice and Dorian, even though she couldn't see them. She was half-crouched on her three outlandish legs. Her wings were at full span, thus signaling that she would fly if ever she freed herself from the Watcher's strength of knowing. Welts appeared on her forearms and her craggy face. The skin beneath her hollowed eyes swelled alarmingly. Membrane under her wings grew puffy as the creature contacted others by impulses that flowed out through the skin.

Presently the Watcher dimmed in Justice's eyes.

She had come to a decision. *Dorian*.

Dorian did not move, but he was ever alert to her. And knew not to anticipate what might happen next.

*You will break contact with me right now, Dorian*.

At once he did so. Without question, he broke off telepathic contact and cut off that sense he had of Justice which was with him at all times. She was protecting him from something, he realized. She being the Power, he would wait for her where he was.

She would now enter the mind of the Slaker, he decided. For there could be no other way to communicate with a being who only vaguely sensed their presence. Never had any one of them entered the mind singly of an unknown creature beyond their time. Justice had first probed Miacis' mind while still part of the unit. Thomas had probed the worlmas, but they were a lower form. To enter the mind of an alien, obviously intelligent being without help from the unit would not be easy.

He settled back to wait out the time it would take Justice. He did not take his eyes off her.

She let the shades of her fear and worry lift

from her. Sallow yellows and grays of her anxious moments drifted away. In their place streamed the summer white light of home. Much of her love was homeward. There was her family, her brothers, before any of them knew of their powers. There was her home town, its people and the quiet life. The accumulated hopes and nightmares of that place would make up a large part of who she was when and if she touched the mind of the Slaker.

She intended entering the flow of the Bambnua's thoughts.

If I'm able to swim with her mind-currents, I'll make contact. Try to at least, she thought. What if they are too beyond anything I'd imagine, what then? What if I have to get out of there fast? Then I wouldn't dare make contact.

She sat cross-legged. Her robe was pulled tightly over her knees and tucked under her feet. The cowl covering her hair kept the dust from her face. Her hands, pressed firmly in her lap, were concealed in the robe sleeves.

Guess I need to see myself all dressed up like this.

A moment later she forgot about it. The Bambnua, the Dustwalker, had become almost calm for the first time since her discovery of Thomas' make-believe cliff. Her third leg had contracted to the level of a stool. And now she actually sat on it. Her wings were folded around her and appeared as solid as armor. Oblong feathers glinted. Her face and head were not concealed. The head was bald, slightly pink, and wet-looking. The Bambnua turned it 180° left, then 180° to the right.

Justice watched with wonderment. *Is it owls I've seen do that?*

She decided it was a frantic movement the Dustwalker made with her head. Around and around the head went, left to right through 360°, as she searched for, sensed, energy she was unable to see. At last, when Justice sat utterly still, the Bambnua homed in on the place.

Justice felt the depth of the Terrij being's glaucous eyes. The grayish-blue cast over the deep green irises was not non-human. It was somehow beyond human.

*Scary,* Justice thought, *and no way to figure what her eyes mean gaping at me like that. Or even if they know how to mean. Well, why don't I get* on *with it?*

She was about to, but she was cautious and rightly so. She would wait five, ten minutes more. See what, if anything, the Bambnua would do through her staring.

*We don't know if she has some true power besides the way she calls her crew to her through her skin. We do know that time is changed when she moves. Is that it? And does she make the* change? Or is it that no change takes place? No interval, I guess you would say.

Justice waited, hoping the Bambnua would jump closer to her, then back, so she could study the strange maneuver up close. But the Terrij did not move in that way. However, she did move.

I don't believe it!

The creature's chin appeared to collapse and fold under the upper jaw beneath the roof of her mouth. That left her nose, eyes and skull exposed, and her nose flattened in on itself. Next her entire head lowered itself onto the first few vertebrae of the neck.

Justice gaped, fascinated. Across from her was a thing that looked like an egg-shaped column of steel, and on top of it was this pale, damp, oval object with two green slits for eyes.

And like a turtle, too. And like an owl! But she's human, Justice thought. Don't you forget that. I wonder can she pivot her head when it's down like that? *Is* it human? I mean, is she? I say she is as human as I am, but maybe she's made wrong. Oh, I'd say she's made very wrong, like everything else around here. Does she have the sense to know? And care to be something else than herself—like I once wanted to be one of my brothers! Or, if not that, to be a grown-up teenage girl? I'll never be a teenager now. May come to look just like one someday, but I'll never ever *be* one.

A flood of memories. A deep, inner sob.

What's come over me? Justice frightened for a moment. Then she found the will to concentrate on the business before her. She stared at the Terrij, who still had her head retracted. She watched for another few minutes. Who could tell what else the Dustwalker was capable of?

Justice glanced around, saw Dorian yards away unmoving. The sight of him was not a comfort. She worried that something might happen to him while she was in mind-touch with the Slaker. What could she do? She did check to see whether more Slakers were at close range. She saw none and sensed that the others were still at a distance.

And flicked her mind. Within a blink of an eye, Justice transferred her mind within the Bambnua's. She plunged into streams of Slaker thought and memory. There was Slaker life and Slaker history—past, present. There was heritage, not just strange. It was fantastic, bizarre.

In one memory, a great colony of Slakers was on the move. Justice gathered that it was on a quest, a long search for an end. In the memory flow, the Quest for an end stood out plainly. But, for Justice, the meaning of it was lost. Then she experienced a steady engagement of thought-pictures.

She felt incredible weight and massive bulk. The Bambnua was heavy and clumsy, walking on three legs, wings at rest. The force of gravity acted on her shifting center of mass. She continually fought to keep her balance against what was for her a relentless pull from the center of the earth. Her movements were dizzying. The maneuvers, or lack of them, were caused by this balance disturbance.

Justice felt like vomiting. The alien motion surrounding her mind became quite sickening. She also discovered a new shape of loneliness. It was a wildness of independence. She knew a lust to live and a ferocious desire to fly. Through the thought-pictures of memory, Justice knew the Bambnua would fly, and soon. Flying was the Dustwalker's way of escaping the torture of her cumbersome bulk on the ground.

Justice, in mind with the Dustwalker's memory, understood that the Bambnua carried a male infant under each wing. The infants were the offspring of an ordinary female Slaker, and they would never fly. The Bambnua carried them because *that* female had dropped them; otherwise, they would be kicked about (kicked about? Justice didn't comprehend and let it go as the stream of memory continued). So the Bambnua had taken the infants under her wings. Safe, out of sight, nestled against her, they breast-fed and curled their toes with satisfaction.

Their contentment was comical. They rolled

their bluish eyes and humped their backs in pleasure. Justice would have laughed out loud if she
hadn't feared the Bambnua might become aware
of her. So far, the Dustwalker had no inkling of
her presence.

Now, in Dustland, where the entities of Justice
and Dorian were invisible to her, the Bambnua sat
as before. Facing Justice, she was aware of something and saw nothing, save Thomas' cliff and
white rock. The power of the unseen energy kept
her still and in one place.

Picture-memory. Justice in the Bambnua's un-
broken mind-streams.

The added weight of the infants under her
wings caused the Bambnua's body to overheat.
Feeling even more ill, Justice fought down nausea.
Suddenly she saw through the Bambnua's sight, a
sweeping 360° view over the whole colony. The
sensation of all those Slakers—there had to be at
least sixty or seventy of them—was terrifying.
Male Slakers were ugly creatures, and powerful.
They had downy hair about an inch long in a pattern along the center of the scalp, like the comb of
a rooster. Their inability to fly caused them occasionally to attack a female attempting a lift-off.

Justice sensed that, bound to the earth, the
males looked on the flying females with growing
intolerance. Within the colony there was an un-
dercurrent of strife between male and female, sep-

arate from the fierceness between male and male. The female of the species had little heart for battle. Her basic struggle was for equilibrium against the force of gravity.

Only for the sake of the whole colony and the Quest did such a being as the Bambnua suffer walking on the ground part of the time with the males. There was not much of a sense of liking or dislike in her for the males. No emotion that could be considered deep caring. There was instinct for protecting colony and kelms. She would do anything short of damaging herself severely, or weakening herself beyond survival, to carry out the Quest for the end.

What is *the end*? Justice sensed that the answer was near.

The Bambnua, the Dustwalker, knew she was important to the Quest and that the fact she could fly was an advantage. She accepted the male as a most important part of the kelm but not necessarily a vital force for the Quest to the end. She accepted other females and the *yun* Slakers, as tikes were called. Yuns. The Bambnua accepted her lot, all of it, except for Dustland.

The Bambnua would leave Dustland. All Slakers would leave. They were constantly on the move in order to leave. Deep in Slaker heritage was the idea of end and out. The Quest had to be for an *end* to Dustland and a way *out* of it.

What? Astonished, Justice's mind reeled.

There's an end to it? A beginning to Dustland? Then we have stumbled in—this really could be someone else's future. But how—?

Suddenly she sensed symbols of Slaker communication. She had missed them entirely, at first, she had been so involved in the Slaker memories. But behind the pictures there were sounds. They were harsh and strident. Their thrust was violent. But slowly, as Justice grew more comfortable with the Bambnua, with the weight of her powerful bulk rushing toward the end, she began to comprehend a small part.

To say that the noise Slakers made was spoken language was to attempt to put whatever it was in terms of her own time. It was not language as Justice knew English. But it was far different from whines or grunts or howls or roars of animals. It was Slaker *phamph-uan*, Justice gathered from a series of thought-pictures. All Slakers communicated in 'ph-uan, and yun Slakers were born knowing it.

There was a way of warning outside of language. Only dustwalkers like the Bambnua had extrasensory ability through the skin. Then Dustwalker must be a category, Justice realized. The colony she was viewing, which consisted of two kelms, had three mature dustwalkers and one on the way.

In a revolving view out of the Bambnua's eyes, Justice searched for a pregnant female, but could not find one. She did discover a female carrying something soft and almost round that was covered with a fine pinkish down.

That's it! Female Slakers lay eggs!

The female Slakers were egg-layers. And this egg-layer who carried the downy egg was also a dustwalker.

But did only dustwalkers lay dustwalker eggs? Justice wondered. Yes. Yes, four to a colony. The dustwalker, the one in the picture carrying the egg, had become infected.

With—digging!

She had been killed.

There came a rapid flow of pictures. Here was heritage of ancient depth. Slakers had come from beneath the dust to live on the surface ground.

They emerged from deep holes and dark tunnels. Slakers believed they had not devised these dank, subterranean places. But they found themselves in them. They grew, raised yuns and continued in them. When they died, they were shunted into short side tunnels, which were sealed when they were full of the dead. In that ancient time they had not eaten the dead.

Then what did they eat? Justice wondered.

Slakers ate things in the ground. Things in the ground.

Until one ancient time there came a Slaker who shivered and grew frightened of the dark. That one's skin erupted in welts. All who had been alive then had felt the skin eruption. And somehow they knew because of it that great change was upon them.

The one, the Slaker, gasped for breath, had to get out of the tunnels. Had to. Wiggling through holes and tunnels for an endless time. Endless. Grew tired, weakened. The pain of the welts; they became infected. The Slaker was a mass of running sores. And died.

But I don't understand—

And died. And the next one to shiver and panic in the dark. Came crawling and wiggling. The time was long. Was long. That one, too, weakened and died of infection. But beside her was found an egg. And the egg lived to become the third one to panic. It realized the huge humps on its back were useless in the tunnels, worthless for crawling, but good for covering and keeping warm. This one, after an agony of time and loneliness, of trial and error through the tunnels, reached the surface ground. She. The first.

Dustwalker?

Justice searched through recent flow of thought.

The one killed not long ago had been caught digging. Thus, she had been brought down from the air by a crew of females. Digging was the action nearest to a crime. Any caught digging, male or female or yun, was killed. Not one Slaker decided this. All of them apparently knew by instinct. This was a law of the kelms, as close as Justice could understand it. Never would Slakers return to the underground. And the dustwalker recently killed had become food for those who lived.

So little food for so many? Justice wondered.

Add to it bodies of two others who had died of natural causes—a fight among five males—and there was blood and flesh enough for the strongest of the colony. The remaining Slakers would feed on what they could find. Small creatures. Perhaps worlmas.

Eagerly, Justice homed in on the picture-thought of worlmas.

Why did some worlmas move when they were dry husks? When they seemed no longer to live? Were the husks another stage of life, like old age?

Sitting there across from the Bambnua but still in the Bambnua's mind, Justice's curiosity had got the better of her. She had suggested the worlma questions to the Bambnua.

She should have known better. It was the first time she had made her mind presence known. Justice had built the questions in pictures as Slakers made picture-thoughts. And had overlooked the very real danger to herself.

Without warning, there came a seething burst of sound that was staggering: WHY YOU WHY? WHYYOUWHY WHY YOU WHY?

Inside the Bambnua's mind, she was trapped in a sickening sensation and jolted in a surge upward, then down, then back up and down as the Terrij vaulted into the air by the strength of her third leg.

The Dustwalker was not trying to take off in flight, but to see above everything, Justice thought, fleetingly. To see over the dust.

The Bambnua broke out in welts, warning off the Slakers at a distance.

Justice felt her skin on fire. Breathtaking pain. She sucked air in, but could not breathe out again. Desperately she tried to get out of the Bambnua's head.

Fire. I'm on Fire. Die.

She truly believed she was dying. Life definitely faded from her. She saw hordes of Slakers tearing her limb from limb. Dead, she was a carcass to be eaten. She found out that death was seeing. It was hearing, but with no ability for life movement. She was devoured. There had been no pain. All was white light where her mind and life had been. White light of Miacis' Star.

Justice fainted dead away.

# 9

___

Seated as before, Justice faced the Dustwalker. But she was still inside the Bambnua's mind. She did not even dare to think. For she was certain that before she had fainted the Bambnua had mind-spoken to her.

Now the Bambnua was in contact with a group of Slakers from her kelm. Although the whole colony was on the move, this was the group that had stayed with her to investigate the source of the energy she had discovered. All of the group were females and loyal to the Bambnua. Being able to fly, they were not concerned about catching up with the colony again.

Cautiously the group had come nearer to Thomas' imaginary cliff. They could see it now, absolutely clear and stark in the dust. They had not come upon the real watering hole yet, because the cliff image was too startling. But they could smell fresh water; it took all of their control not to rush to it. They were perpetually at the edge of maddening thirst. The Slakers waited upon the Bambnua's consent. And they trusted her completely in matters of extrasensory and the protection of the colony.

Picture-thought. Commands from the Bambnua to the female Slakers:

danger. wait.

The group halted for as long as was necessary. Justice sensed them—wings touching, and heads resting on one another's shoulders. Like giant birds sleeping.

Apparently the Bambnua felt that grave danger was still present and she would hold back her females until she figured out what to do. She had not connected the danger in her mind to the energy still at rest across from her.

Justice knew she had severely frightened the Dustwalker by entering her thought with the question about worlmas. It had been dumb of her. She had indeed felt as if she were dying and had been happy, exhilarated when she came to again. But maybe what she had done wasn't as dumb as she had first thought. That slight mind-touching might have paved the way. The next time the Bambnua might not respond with so much fear.

Oh, yes, I'll do it again, Justice thought, careful to keep the thought confined to herself. That woman said something to me, I know she did, if

I could just think what it was. All that sickness came on me so fast. And then that awful burning.

Now Justice realized she would have to work quickly before the Bambnua brought in the other females. Even with what had happened, she sensed that, given a proper preparation, this female and the others would not deliberately harm her.

I could be wrong, she thought. But it's my guess that these poor women are more gentle than they want the male Slakers to find out. Well, I won't ever tell on them!

The Bambnua's mind was not powerful in the way that Justice's was. Yet Justice had experienced force and might like nothing she had known. She knew what she had felt was mature and womanly, in the same way her mother was grown-up and womanly, and the way she herself would one day be a grown-up woman. With the Bambnua, that female force held a sense of agony and struggle of the very first dustwalker, as well as all others down through time. And, touching the Bambnua's thoughts, Justice had in herself felt courageous and bold.

Justice had the power, was the Watcher. She would make contact with the Bambnua, letting it be understood that she could sense and project with greater strength than all of the dustwalkers together from the beginning of time. If her power was not clear to the Bambnua when the Bambnua realized her there in her thoughts, then it would be necessary for Justice to reveal it. The process would have to be undertaken with care, and slowly.

Slowly. Slowly, Justice thought. I do still hold the balance? I am still the Power? Yes. Yes, I will always be the Watcher.

Slowly she filtered the summer through the Bambnua's mind. The sweet white light of her dear home, the same white light that had come when she thought she was dead.

The Bambnua surged and shuddered at Justice's touch. She raged with fire, about to break out in welts again. But this time Justice held on in the Bambnua's mind. With hard will, she fought down the Dustwalker's alarm signals.

The Bambnua began to shake all over, but she did not surge or shudder. She was tight as a drum within. She shook. She watched within this new presence with a mixture of fear and glaring bravery.

The sweet white light was warm with the scent of clover.

All that Justice knew and loved. Her family. Her brothers. The town. Its people and animals. Vivid hopes and nightmares. The summer sun and sweltering nights—so little dust! The town pool. Kids shining in the clover surrounding the pool and browned to a burning dampness. Sweat running down backs and armpits. Truly sweet scent of chlorine. Bright and sudden image of the summer field in back of Justice's home. Then, diving splashes in the pool. The wonderful weight of water as shoulders, heads, cut through the shimmering aqua. There is the wading pool and the squeals of babies delighting in the coolness.

Yuns. Baby-yuns, thought Justice.

The Bambnua quivered down her backbone and to the tips of her wings.

And came her supreme effort to mind-speak:

YA HA NAS  WHYYOU  BHA HA BHA HEES

There it is. *There it is!*

BHA HE BHES A deep struggle. Bravery over fear from the Bambnua.

Babies! And you said, Why You.

YOUWHYYOU  BHA  HEBHES

Oh, wait! Listen—oh, see the pictures!

The Bambnua, the Dustwalker, was no longer frightened. All of her defenses gave way to her extraordinary curiosity. Her desire to know was overwhelming and ingrained in her makeup. The more she was able to learn, the better the chance for the Quest to find the end. All thought-processes led finally to this ancient, urgent desire.

Justice began. Thought-pictures of her own, and as gentle as she could make them.

Lazy days. Lovely star-filled nights. No moon.

The new moon. The passage of time. Time and Justice. Her brothers and time. Justice growing up with her brothers. The coming of their power. An unending sadness. Resignation.

We have come together, she pictured to the Bambnua. We are the first unit. We are joined, my brothers, the boy here called Dorian and I. As you are joined with your colony. We are the unit. Past. Time and travel. Out of our time, we come here to your time. We come from along-ago past time. We time-travel. We are powerful. Do not be afraid of us. But we are powerful. We can move things. We can move you. We can move almost anything. Greetings, Terrij, Bambnua- Walker.

A series of pictures in which Justice and her brothers learn to use the power. Dorian's mother, the Sensitive, takes time in secret teaching them to fine-tune their energy. They form the unit at Justice's direction. As the unit, the three boys and she use less power more efficiently. There is far less strain on the anatomy and mind of each of them with the same good effect.

Rambling scenes—pictures of life back home, which are surrounded by Justice's mind at work. There comes a parade of these, Justice's thoughts.

The Bambnua sights the rambling scenes and moves her mind-sensations through them. It's as if she can walk through a moving-picture show.

She focuses on the strange sounds coming from within the scenes.

Projecting her thoughts within the scenes Justice is thinking.

I figured out that my own folks are the last generation. But I don't mean the last of people, just the last time people are born without some power. I figure that when my brothers and I and Dorian were born the way we were, others around the world were born the same. Had to be, don't you think?

No longer did the Bambnua quiver or shake. She hummed within while holding herself still and fast. Tight as a high wire, humming, she saw through Justice's pictures.

From now on, Justice continued, each of the generations will bring more *us* of power. Just a few. Always only a few—like there're always only a few dustwalkers, you.

*You and me*, tracing, *we're not so different. We are the few.*

The Bambnua, filled with sensing, with feeling and waking. The hum was the machinery of her becoming. As one time Justice had become something more than herself, so the Dustwalker was becoming new.

The moving-picture scenes revealed clouds and hills. Greenery. Honeysuckle. Lilac. Winged creatures.

The Bambnua ceased to hum inside. She watched a flight of ducks winging against the dark swell of winter clouds. Saw their shape, heard the sound of their squawking. Admired the formation and their swiftness through air.

Justice felt a suffocating longing. It took her sense for a moment. Then the Bambnua hummed, stronger than ever. Justice fought back her own longing for home.

*Someday, home, the few of us of power will find the way of sensing others like us and come together faster. And never again the long time it took the Sensitive to find me. Dorian's mom, searching, taking months and months and not even sensing me. But finally, holding to this tiny, teeny scent of power off somewhere. That was me! A little bitty scent, almost lost forever in the wide old world!*

YOUMVE     YOUMVE.

The Bambnua, surging inside.

MVEMVE     YOU

A wild siege of becoming.

MVEMVEMVE     YOUYOU Screaming, a raging out of control.

*Wha . . . what?* Justice holding on.

MVEYOU

*What?* Like a whisper.

MVEYOUMVEYOUMVEYOU

Mve you? *Move you?*

*Move you! Move you! I said it. I said we could*

*move anything, the unit could. . . . You've been
studying that while I ran my mouth.*

Justice was stunned. So unexpected the Bambnua's understanding was. It made her human,
surely.

*Move you, that's what you want. I said it. With
my power. Yes, sure. Sure! Dorian!*

Swiftly, Justice removed her mind from the
Bambnua's. She was as before, seated across from
the Dustwalker; this time her mind was where it
was supposed to be.

Dorian came quickly beside her. The Bambnua felt this source of energy.

Justice mind-traced: *She wants a demonstration.*

*You mean, you've been able to reach her by
telepathy?* Dorian traced.

*What do you think I've been doing all this time?
I gave her scenes from home. Brother! About made
me cry, too, just remembering and picturing it all.*

*I know it,* he traced. *It happens to me here,
too.*

*Anyway, she must've been studying the way I
made the pictures because, the next thing I knew,
she was speaking back at me, back to my thoughts.*

*Wow! And could you get any of her language?*
he wanted to know.

*I guess I must've. I'm not sure. First I was in
her picture-stream of things gone by, and then*

*more recent memories. But if it's language, it's sure different from anything I've heard of. Is it language we think in? Or is it pictures put into words? But I've reached her. Dorian, we can get going with it.*

*What's the demonstration to be?* he traced.

*She wants to be moved.* A stunned silence from Dorian. *She wants us to move her around. She can't see us. But I had thought to her that we could move just anything, the unit could. And did she take that to heart! Now she wants us to move* her!

Dorian made no answer, but prepared himself for the demonstration. He was bound to Justice with mutual strength held in common. Never was their mutuality as powerful as the binding of the unit when the four of them were joined. Yet it was force enough. Their combined effort could carry the Bambnua, Dustwalker.

*What a name—such a sound it has,* Dorian traced.

Then Justice closed down all tracings. The Watcher filled their intelligences. The two of them descended far within to deliver their irresistible strength to the surface of themselves. From the inner depths rose their force. They focussed it on the Bambnua. Divined that she wanted to move in one direction. Up.

The Terrij felt herself being moved. At once she reversed the process that had lowered her head on the neck vertebrae. Her head came up, and slowly her collapsed chin unfolded from under the roof of her mouth. Her flattened nose was prominent again. She had not lifted a wing. Still in a seated position on her retracted third leg, she rose.

It might have been strong winds of Rollers that caused her to rise. But there was no wind. Yet she was lifted up and up.

MVE  MVE  YOUYOU  MVE  Thought-spoken in rhythm with the pulse-beat of her brave and daring blood.

For the first time Dorian was in touch with the alien Slaker. All of her strange other-being, which Justice had known before him, he knew now. He would have faltered if not for the Watcher there. He was part of the Watcher as well as Justice. He was more closely tuned with It than when all of them were the unit. A clarity of light and knowledge was his senses. He heard the Bambnua mind-speak: MVE  MVE  And understood as Justice had.

She, the Bambnua-Walker, rose so high that other Slakers on the ground, waiting just out of sight, quickly lost her contact. They were lost to her. For one time in her life—her long, long life; its vigorous phase was longer than a century—she was adrift. And free of all her colony. No longer could she sense kelm or the female crew through her skin. She did not care to be their warning of danger, or their scout for food and water. The need to lead one more Slaker or to find one last watering hole was lost.

Because.

Above the Bambnua, dust grew bright. And brighter. The Dustwalker shook out her wings.

She had never hoped. She went through motions of searching for an end by instinct. What else did she live for in the dust of suffering? But now all that had changed. Since the moment she had sensed that trail of energy unlike anything anywhere in the dust place, she had dared to hope. And, at last coming upon that which remained invisible but powerful, she had sensed what it could do for her. Times, traveling the land, when she vaguely sensed its limits. Now she comprehended what this new, invisible energy might do for her.

MVE     YOUYOU     MVEMVEMVE

*Now. Rise. Rise.*

Suddenly she was blinded by light. Screeching with pain from the brilliant, warm light. She covered her cruddy eyes with her wings. And crouched on air so free of dust. Her eyes teared and burned until the moment came when she could bear the sharp, piercing pain. She peeked through her feathers. She was holding still on absolutely clear air.

Here. There. The enormous world of light. Blue above and beyond.

They gave the name to her. *Sky.*

She shuddered once, knowing the energy that had lifted her was also in her mind. It was one and the same. But she was brave. And soon she did not tremble. She did not move for ever so long a time. Until she mind-spoke.

SA KA SASA KAA A sigh of ancient yearnings. SAKA SAKA

*Yes. Sky.*

Throughout the vast light was the blue. All was clear and blue. Serene.

She need not bounce up on her third leg. She simply lifted her great wings and took off from the band of energy.

And soared.

On an immense silence of sky and light the Bambnua floated and glided until she had sailed down near the dust again. There she again rose on her wingpower, straight up. She gave off a deep and steady tone that vibrated with ageless feeling throughout the blue. It was a hawking swell. A Slaker song of praise, the first one ever.

"HAWHAW! YA! HAWA! HAWHAW! YAWHA! WAWA! WA!"

On the ground, they pulled back their power. They traced to one another again.

*She sure doesn't need us now*, came from Dorian.

They concentrated through the dust, upward, to where the Bambnua flew with grace all on her own.

*Soon she'll need us again*, Justice traced.

*You afraid she's gonna fall? I don't think she will, not the way*—Dorian stopped, suddenly aware that the Slaker's falling was not what concerned Justice. With their extrasensory, Justice held fast to the Bambnua.

For the Dustwalker was searching for the end to Dustland. She had taken off in a straight line, away from the point on the ground where Justice and Dorian waited. And, imperceptibly, her line was curving.

*She's turning*, traced Dorian. *Shouldn't we do something—?*

Justice was intent on the Bambnua far above. She listened, and saw.

The Dustwalker had her sensory locked on their energy still touching her. From it, she had headed straight away. As far as she knew, she was still headed straight away, with no inkling that gradually she was curving in a great arc to the left.

They were certain she had been near something, the edge, perhaps, of Dustland. But she had no idea how close she had come. To her mind, she was continuing in a straight line above the dust. And from her view, Dustland appeared to be without end.

Times when silence was a clearer sign than mind-tracing. And now Justice was utterly silent. The Watcher was with them; yet Dorian thought to shield his mind. He did not question why the need of shields. But, from Justice's manner, he knew to close off his thought to himself. From within he gathered that the Bambnua slowly turned and did not know it. She meant to go straight to find the end, but she could not, or would not. He assumed she would willingly go straight to the end if she could.

Not even with shields in place and from deep within would Dorian think the next thought.

The Bambnua-Walker was flying faster and faster. Frantic, she searched for the end. No longer did it occur to her that the end would be the way out for all Slakers. Her total strength was concentrated on the effort of flying.

The power of Dorian and Justice combined with the Watcher stayed close by her, but out of her way. She grew tired. Slowly her body sagged downward toward the dust. Her wings flapped, but with less force, until at last they could no longer move at all.

She plummeted. The extrasensory of the two of them was there to ease her way. She drifted down through the dust. Choking and gagging. So clean had been her breathing awhile ago. Always she would remember the blue, although she could not name it.

*I am the Watcher*, spoke in the Bambnua. *The color is blue. Do not lose hope now that you've found it. Perhaps someday you will have the blue again.*

The Bambnua could not comprehend all of it. Yet she felt a warmth of sympathy. But again she despaired. Exhausted, she hugged the hardened, dusty earth as Justice and Dorian let her gently down.

She was a heap of feathers from which came ragged breaths of "Ah-unnah . . . hunn-ah." She spun on the ground and was on her back, both wings extended.

*Fallen angel*, Dorian traced as the Watcher dimmed from his and Justice's eyes.

They watched as welts rose on the Bambnua's skin. She summoned her crew. She did not make a move. She lay there, a forlorn and absurd sort of bird, Justice observed. An ugly, pathetic, beached bird.

*Yes, a fallen one*, Justice suddenly traced to Dorian. *I think she's awfully brave to work so hard.*

Now there came the Slakers who had waited out of sight the whole time because the Terrij had commanded them to. She had called them and they came. They feared the unseen power. They felt it mightily, but they came on.

Justice and Dorian watched as the female creatures crept to the Bambnua in burst of being in one place, then the next. Justice noted how light on their feet they seemed, when she knew the difficulty they had keeping their balance. Not a sound did they make as their huge wings caressed the air in fear. Each one swayed on three legs, coming forth with no visible change of space. They surrounded the Bambnua. They were seated. Were lying down. Stretched out on their backs, as was their Terrij. They positioned themselves however the Bambnua did. She was stretched out. They stretched out. In a flick of an eye she was standing. They were standing.

Dorian had had no premonition that the Bambnua was about to stand. He sensed no change of space or position.

*The first of anything I haven't been able to mind-read all along,* Justice traced.

*I think it's real spooky,* Dorian traced back. *I can't get a fix on when any one of them will move.*

*That's the only thing you can't read about them?* Justice wanted to know. *I mean, now that I've told you all I know and you've been in contact?*

*The only thing,* Dorian traced. *And that's because, I swear, because the moves happen in another dimension.*

*Wish they were*, Justice traced. *Then we'd never know everything about them.*

*What do you mean by that?*

*I mean, I'm glad not to know it all—don't we always know too much? And it's not another dimension.*

*What makes you so sure?* No sooner had Dorian asked than he had the answer. She divined it—read it, sensed it, as was her way.

*It's their power*, she traced lightly, like the softest mental touch. *Oh, they must've had it all along, from the time the first one of them came up from underground. Maybe something down there could harm them if it saw them moving—ooh!—I'm not sure about that part. I can't find that part anywhere, so I'm figuring it out. Making it up is what I'm doing, I guess. Anyway, they have it. That little amount of mind-control. Nothing can see them move. They blanket the whole area with that quick, sharpened force. Thought I felt an instant of something funny every time she ended up in another place. It was movement I felt but couldn't see. So quick and smooth I almost missed it. Did miss it all of this time.*

*Wow!*

*But I'm glad they have something to themselves.*

*Sounds like you're tired of what we have*, he traced.

*I'm weary of it right now, I think. Never had*

*to know some souls as sad as these Slaker folks
right there in front of us.*

The females had gathered in around their
Bambnua. All laid their bald heads on one another's shoulders. Each standing on three legs, not
one of them displaced. But the whole crew of them
swayed in a slow, somber sweep to and fro. They
jibbered in peculiar bursts of sounds. Once spoken, the sounds slid heavily down to the dust, as
if the weight of utterances brought them down.

Quickly the crew knew that their Terrij had
risen and flown above the dust. Knew that she
had searched and found that the miserable land
had no end.

But that new energy which had moved the
Bambnua on high—it could move all of them
above the dust, could it not? They wanted to know.

Their Terrij did not have the answer to that.
And what did it matter, since the dust had no end?

At this moment of deepest lament, Justice entered again the mind of the Terrij and the minds
of her crew.

I am the Watcher. Trust the Bambnua. She
knows. The Bambnua trusts me. I know what she
does not. We will help you find the end.

Slakers lifted their heads and turned simul-
taneously to stare at the empty space in front of
them. They watched it for a long, long time.

And through the silence came noise from far

away. It grew, bringing heavy waves of dust. The air blew in a wind before Justice and Dorian realized a Roller was coming.

*Must be one!* traced Dorian. *But where to hide?*

*Wait.* Justice watched the Slakers.

They had not moved. But they were shorter. Leaning backward on their third legs, they became shorter. The third legs were being driven, jammed into the ground as anchors. Wedged deep below the dust, twisted in and jammed so they could not be moved by Rollers.

*A* Jam *people—that's what it means!*

*Sure*, traced Justice. *They've had plenty of time to find ways of keeping safe from Rollers. But wait.*

She listened. The thick dust lightened as it had high above when the Bambnua had risen. It was thinning, Justice was quick to note. The air around them became nearly clear. The ground grew bare. Off at a distance came a black sheet of dust higher and higher through the air. Then a pulling at her began, like a suction. It let up before it could move her or Dorian.

The Slakers stayed still, anchored as they were, with chins resting on one another's shoulders. Silent, rheumy eyes closed—how old could they be? The Bambnua-Walker had welted again, contacting the rest of her kelm.

A crashing swoosh came from within the wall

of dust. The sound took them by surprise. Dorian leaped up in a run in the opposite direction.

*Wait!* Justice warned. *It can't hurt our minds.*

*Well, it sure looks like it can. And as long as I've got this body, I'm getting out of here.*

*Dorian, you come right back!*

Reluctantly he came back, and they waited as the booming dust commenced to fall in shrouds. A sheet of it spread out over the ground in ripples. Dust rose around them, as murky as it had been before the Roller came.

Out of the dust where the Roller had been stepped Miacis. Standing upright, she was taller than Justice would have dared imagine. She half-dragged Thomas and half-carried Levi. Justice didn't have a moment even to be stunned. For Miacis opened her muzzle and began speaking.

"Greetings, Master Lady!" Her brand-new voice had the gentle resonance of a harp. "I bring you two good old boys, ain't got no better sense. Oh, yes!"

Speechless, Justice stared at the giant golden animal. Suddenly she grinned and nodded her satisfaction. But Levi was still on her mind, and she hurried over to him.

"He not so happy," Miacis said, releasing Levi. "He a pretty sick runaway from home."

"Thomas made him run," Justice said. "Levi would never have done it!"

She and Dorian took hold of Levi between them. He was conscious and happy to see them.

Justice traced to him, *Don't you worry. We're leaving right away.*

Miacis still had hold of Thomas. She let him slide to the ground. Looking at Justice, she chuckled, as only a talking beast full of surprise knew how.

"This here is some character brother, Master," she purred. "This escaper better take a tip from me." Her hind leg nudged Thomas toward the Slakers.

He hadn't taken his eyes from the monstrous winged things before him. He crawled back toward Miacis. Never had Thomas dreamed of such huge, ugly shapes—with wings, no less—could you beat that? And crusted over with dirt and filth. He scooted to Miacis. She was easier to take than the winged monsters.

"Boy, you runaway is sure some chickenshit!" Miacis yelled.

"Miacis," Justice said.

Miacis had her gleaming blind eyes on the Slakers, recognizing their scent. She had come in contact with them all of her life. Her fur bristled with contempt.

"Hi you was, dusty roaders?" she said.

Slakers stared, listening to her animal voice.

"You creeps!" Miacis smirked. "Ain't never goin' find way home. Might as well fly away, Jammers. Ain't no home. Who need it? Not me, boy. Me got dust and rolling. Fine place, this disaster. Good ole' city. Fine master, too."

"Miacis, be still!" This time the Watcher echoed through Justice's voice.

Miacis lowered herself from her height and lay down before Justice. "Yes, Master." She simpered.

"Call me Justice!"

Miacis stayed quiet. She blinked her fiery eyes and wondered for the thousandth time if the master was Star.

But Star never say anything to Miacis, she thought. This Master commanding any minute. Nope. Don't think this one be Star. Master always tell me how. She going to take off for her city now.

*Let's get out of here*, traced Dorian.

*Thomas. Levi*, Justice traced. There was no hesitation from either one of them. Quickly all of them joined minds. All felt the strength and order of being the unit. The depth of it was even to all.

i am the Watcher.

The unit was all and i. It fixed its gaze on Miacis, who sat still and serene before it. Its watching was a resplendent glowing.

i leave you now, great Miacis.

Miacis blinked at the infeeling of no-sound and no-voice. She held still, purring. Stillness, silence was her way at the time of parting.

*You will return, First Unit?* she traced easily.

i will return. Join with me tighter now to the moment of Crossover.

The unit locked in tighter the mind-to-mind it kept with Miacis. It knew and reckoned the pulse of her animal being.

i am the Watcher.

It turned its whelm of watching on the Slakers, who now stood on all three legs, as the danger of Rollers had passed. Such power as was the unit had force against which they could rest their heavy bulk. They leaned into the energy. And it flowed over them.

Your Quest is nearly over, Bambnua, Dust-walker. i will return.

The Bambnua keened, uttering harsh cries. Her old eyes searched upward through the dust as the energy, the great power flowed away until it had disappeared out of the land.

She had lost the mighty force for now. This she jabbered to her crew. Swiftly she shifted her thoughts and told the females to drink from the pool of fresh water. At once the females were beside the pool. They were wading in. They were drinking. They had drunk. The Bambnua drank. She lay on the water, wings spread. She sank. A long moment and she was back on top of the water. She was out of it.

The Terrij, the Bambnua, welted, calling her kelm. The kelm was on the range with the colony. They would note the whereabouts of such splendid liquid.

She had taken notice that the cliff and rock had faded the moment the great unseen power had vanished. She stared at nothing, jibbering to herself, sounds falling at her feet. All of the crew followed her lead, jibbering. The Dustwalker leaned back on her third leg. She flew. They all flew. And, flying, they were gone.

The unit hung suspended on the seam between future and the Crossover. In a lightning probe, it was aware of turbulence ahead where commenced the Crossover. It felt Miacis about to pull back her mind, leaving the unit.

*I await your return, First Unit.* Mind-tracing in the last instant with a delicate purring.

i am the Watcher. i will return.

Miacis was detached from the unit. *Master!*

Miacis was gone.

The unit left the future and plunged into the Crossover. It was a writhing, spiraling condition between times. It was not yet a present event.

# 10

It could never be sure it would get back home precisely where it should. It had focused its power-of-being on the chestnut tree. And it imagined the scent of that shade buckeye, where the real, breathing bodies of Dorian, Thomas, Levi and Justice sat beneath its branches, hands joined.

The turbulence of the Crossover between future and past echoed with sighs and whispers of mind-travelers come and gone. Gradually the unit came to know that multi-beings infested the Crossover in mental swarms. The t'beings, as Justice and the others would come to call them, had at one time been individual mind-travelers. But the individual had failed to hold its concentration while completing the mind-jump from one time to another. Trapped in the no-end and no-start between times, it would never again find the way back to its proper moment. An individual found others like itself caught in the Crossover. It and the others cooperated, joined and became multi-beings gathered in base swarms to capture new individual time-travelers. In this way, t'beings intended to become strong enough to fix on some *place*. Forever without bodies, they could well become power on the loose to cause havoc at any time.

Justice had divined early on that she, Thomas, Levi and Dorian had best become a unit for strength of mind and self-defense. And the unit had been lucky not to have been uncovered by t'being swarms until the return trip on the second time-travel to the future. The unit knew by then not to lose its concentration, nor break connection with the single obsession it had in mind: getting home. And now the unit whirled and dived, dodging the swarms. It massed its psyche on the past and home. The Watcher observed for it in the anti-where of the Crossover, surrounding it with utmost attention and clear purpose. This the Watcher accomplished while the unit held fast and dared not dream. Only once was the Watcher seriously challenged. A foot-wide swarm drove a wedge of ferocious need into the Watcher's first level of awareness.

*I will have you me*, warned the swarm, with unflagging force.

The unit streaked and dived. It outmaneuvered the swarm, and felt safe enough to indulge in longing for home. It pondered whether it would arrive *in time.* It lengthened and shortened its worrying *in no time.* Laughed inwardly at the confusion words caused itself. It thought it might be losing its mental balance, that perhaps the t'beings had got through the Watcher. It laughed again, this time at how foolish it was to transmit itself through the non-dimension of Crossover. It cried out against the fierce turbulence. It worried that it might not have the strength of mind to set itself free. For an anti-moment it lost faith, it loosened its hold on its proper place and instant in the past. It felt it was doomed.

But the Watcher was true, was power. It guided. The Watcher lit the unit's way through flights of ideas and awful misconceptions. Through the anti-where of nothing, the Watcher never wavered, never did not know.

Until the unit experienced the sweet sensation of cool hand holding cool hand. The Watcher was incandescence as It felt the weight of children's flesh and bone.

Bodies, alive again!

The unit opened its eyes on lands teeming with life and sound and odor. Its mouths filled with saliva at the overpowering scents. It gagged. But soon the discomfort passed as its stomachs settled down. Still the unit could not comprehend much around it. It recognized little. It gazed up into darkness. Saw a far light. It came to know the light. The moon was shining down, fleeing behind swift clouds.

At last the unit had come to its proper time and place. But all was night, with periodic rains. Winds came up over the Trace lands, warm and wet, sweeping tall weeds. The winds brought pouring rain before they and the rains died down again.

i am the Watcher, willed the unit.

The Watcher faded from its eyes. Its mind separated into conscious and unconscious conditions—four of them—one sentient condition for each child. As the separation process took place, the Watcher sensed that Thomas touched It and persuaded It toward himself. The Watcher chose to ignore this proposition. It would keep within the child Justice as the balance for all.

Thomas released the hands he held. They all dropped their hands and slumped back against the tree trunk. They were cold, shivering and wet. The tree branches dripped on them. They were uncomfortable and afraid. They were also relieved, but still frightened, with the Crossover not yet out of their minds.

One of them whimpered and sobbed uncontrollably for a short time. It was Thomas. None of them thought it strange that so strong and, sometimes, so bad a boy should cry. One of them usually did on the return. One crying was a kind of release for all.

Justice put her hand on his shoulder. All of them pulled close, feeling the sudden pain of sore muscles, until Thomas ceased crying. He was at once uncomfortable with them. The next moment he could not tolerate any of them touching him, particularly Justice. That was all right. Thomas was Thomas. Whatever he was; good or bad, much of both or more of one than the other, he was one of them.

"Th-that w-was aw-awful," he whispered, speaking of the Crossover. He realized he had stuttered. In the present he always stuttered, unless he was drumming or tracing.

"But the best was that the Watcher got us through," Justice said.

"B-but b-being helpless l-l-like that!" Thomas said. "W-weee have to-to s-st-stop it. One-ce we're l-locked in con-concen-t-tration, an-any-th-thing can g-get t-t-to us."

"But the Watcher—," she began.

*Damn the Watcher!* he traced, in order to speak more quickly. *You can't keep doing this!*

Yet he knew she could keep doing whatever she wanted to do. The Watcher, although It was for all of them, was hers. Like some shining light turning on and off, It came from her genes. It was immense, unlike anything in the life of minds. And It was willful, just as Justice was.

"I was sure them t'beings was going to get us,"

Dorian said. "I'm scared they'll follow us back here sometime. Could it happen?"

"It could," Justice said, "if they follow our energy flow closely enough. I'll think about that before we go to the future again." At once she was sorry she'd had to mention going. "Thomas, believe me, I don't want to go either, not really."

*I don't want to think about it,* he traced to her. *Just let's get home.*

But none of them moved. They all had felt someone creeping near. In no time they knew it was the Sensitive, Dorian's mother. She must have been frantic when they hadn't returned in daylight. And she had waited, terrified they would not make it back, guarding their flesh and blood all through the night.

"Come on in, Mrs. Jefferson," Justice called out beyond the shield the tree branches made, sweeping low to the ground. Justice smiled in the dark.

Mrs. Jefferson came, her feet smacking through wet grasses.

"Shoo! Shoo!" she cried out as she came. For there were snakes all around them. There were snake beds throughout the Quinella Trace lands. Garter snakes had lived, raised young ones and died here for as long as anyone could remember.

Mrs. Jefferson stooped low and came through the branches. "Child!" she said. "Chil'ren!" She grabbed Justice's hand, and Dorian around the neck. She hugged and kissed her only child, Dorian, as if he'd been gone a lifetime.

"Aw, Mom!" he said, sounding like the boy he was. Yet he did not pull away from his mother, and barely managed to hide the smile of happiness on his face.

Mrs. Jefferson released Justice and Dorian to grab and pump Thomas' hand. He pulled back from her as far as he could against the tree trunk. Mrs. Jefferson grabbed anyway. "Glad to have you back, son," she said, her voice husky with feeling.

Thomas said not a word to her. He did not speak to her if he could help it. He would not speak and stutter and have her think she was better than he was. She, in turn, didn't take to heart his disrespect, this Number One Child, as she called Thomas. But she was mindful lest he harm the Justice child or his brother, the Number Two Child. Number One Child could be dangerous, she was sure of it. Yet, so far, bloodlines and the power of the Watcher held him in check.

Mrs. Jefferson turned her attention to Levi, lying so still. His languid pose spoke to her of illness.

"Oh, child!" she said, grabbing both his hands in hers. "I rubbed these stone-cold hands and arms till I thought to rub they skin off. Had to keep the blood circulating, had to. And 'bout had the worst time to keep the blood warm. Goodness to mercy, you scared me to death not half an hour ago!" She pictured again his shallow breathing, his burning skin and how his eyes had stared wide and empty when the hand-chain had been broken.

Now she saw that he perspired. His skin was almost cool.

Levi grinned at her. "Thanks for everything," he said softly. "It's good to be back home."

"Well, then, let's get yall ready," she told them. "It's the middle of the night. Comin' dawn not too far from now, too."

"The same dawn of our leaving?" Dorian wanted to know.

"Couldn't be," said Justice. "Has to be a day or two later."

"Oh, Lawd," Mrs. Jefferson said. "Been most of twenty-four hour—dawn of yestiddy. Yall recall how you did come out here before even the sun was 'bout up. And that day. And the night come down and rain clouds gatherin'. I said to mysel' to get on down here, see if yall was still all right. I wasn't worryin' mysel', exactly, but I keep getting this feeling that I ought to get down here. So I comes down in the full dark of nine o'clock at night. Shouldn't be dark by then. Know it shouldn't. But they be rain clouds. Rain not come down yet. But it's thunderin' and thinkin' on it. And I hurry on down. Not mindin' for thunder or lightnin', nothing. Just had to make it down here and fast. And rightful I did, too. Mercy. Found Number One"—pointing at Thomas—"clutched up as tight to that water as he could get himsel'. On his knees, and I ain't lyin'. On his knees! Like he was to hide behind the air if that was possible. And the other one, Number Two"—pointing at Levi—"right over there, his eyes wide open and starin' on the dark. And scare me so. I lifted them boys single-handed, tremblin' even in my throat, too. And laid 'em out right back here under this tree again. Done broke the chain of hands, yes they did. And I join the chain back. Didn't know if and when you might be tryin' to get home. Knew you couldn't get home without the hands be joined. And scare me so again, when hours and hours do pass. I thought yall never was coming home. So I'm 'bout to leave here for some blankets to cover yall. And started off, too. I like to died, wonderin' how'm I to explain four empty-headed bodies sittin' holdin' hands in the dark under a shade tree. Glory. Glad I never had to ask somebody to come on down here and he'p me with them corpses!"

They stared at her, struck by the picture she had drawn of their deaths. Empty-headed bodies! But they were thankful for her. Justice tried to get up, and Mrs. Jefferson was there to help.

"We'll start with you, baby-child, oh, Justice, since you always be the most anxious."

She lifted Justice up on her legs, only to see them buckle with no strength. Mrs. Jefferson took hold of Justice before she could fall again. "Now," she said. "Lean on me. We gone take one little-bitty step at a time, that's all they is. Just one at a time."

The Sensitive carried Justice's weight until Justice could feel pinpricks of sensation that forced her up on her toes.

"Ooh! Oh, man, brother, let me sit down," Justice cried.

"Chile, you keep on walkin' or you won't walk no more. We got to get on outta here pretty soon now."

"It feels like my backbone is turned to wood!" Justice moaned.

But it was not long before she and the Sensitive were helping Thomas and Dorian to their feet. The boys stood the pain of leg cramps quite well. An awful cramp curled Thomas' toes under. Justice had to take his foot between her hands and massage it.

"Here, let me do that," Mrs. Jefferson said, taking hold of Thomas.

He telepathed a truce to Mrs. Jefferson. Not in so many words, but in attitude. His attitude spoke volumes to her and it was not necessary for her to read his mind. A relaxation of her face muscles gave her agreement. She and Thomas would get along for the greater good, as long as it was possible. It upset Levi when the two of them argued or nearly came to blows.

All felt the urgency of what they must do for Levi. But they must be in condition themselves before they began it. All would need to pull together for Levi. And Thomas was still up too high, too agitated, to work out effectively.

Wish he'd get rid of some of that hatefulness he come back here with, Mrs. Jefferson thought. She was careful to veil her thinking from Thomas and the rest of them. How come he got to be so bitter all the time? *Who gone allow him near the Two Child with him bein' so hateful?* The Sensitive never could keep her thoughts and the art of tracing separate.

Thomas had sensed her thinking and had caught her tracing. *You shut up!* he traced back. *Just shut up. And why do you have to give with that phoney Southern accent? We know you can talk just as regular as anybody. So why do you have to pretend?*

*Not pretendin' nothin'*, Mrs. Jefferson traced. *Maybe I do it as a reminder to you of what has gone before—humm? Your origins, so to speak. Not to forget them. Past is important. You take the past on along with you to the future, don't you, Number One?*

*I never take it anywhere*, Thomas traced. *I am*

*taken under force. And whatever is in me when I go also goes through force.*

*Times when we all have to cooperate,* she traced.

*But I have a right not to want to cooperate,* Thomas traced. *I have a right to say no, I won't play.*

*Times when one for one is not enough,* traced the Sensitive serenely. *Times when two be one, when three be one is better. But best come the only way, come when all be for one.*

*Yeah, sure. The unit,* he traced. *I know I have no civil rights. I'm enslaved! But give me a cigarette and I'll help you with Lee.* Smirking.

The Sensitive drew back.

*I know you have them,* Thomas traced. *Give me one, I need a cigarette!*

*Give it to him,* came a tracing. It was Justice. *Give him what he needs to calm him down, Mrs. Jefferson.*

*He don't need nothin', makin' out how he's so trapped.*

*But he is trapped,* Justice traced. *We are all trapped.*

*And that's what I mean,* came the Sensitive, right back. *How he gone be more so trapped than anybody else? We all trapped with the gift. Be trapped to know what lies ahead. Cain't none of us let the sensory go. Know how to see and to see again; and not a one of us be able to let loose of it.*

*So give me a cigarette*, traced with a less heavy humor. Letting them know his feelings always seemed to ease Thomas. *I better look after Lee for you now.*

*Right*, Justice traced.

None of them could see into the human structure the way Thomas could. And he could read his identical's flesh and blood without fail. It was necessary that Thomas treat Levi after every Crossover.

"Give Thomas a cigarette," Justice commanded.

Without another word, the Sensitive produced a pack from the folds of her skirt.

Thomas, smoking, seated himself cross-legged under the buckeye next to Levi, who had lain in the same place for almost twenty-four hours. Occasionally Lee rolled his head from side to side. Otherwise he lay still and outwardly showed little discomfort. Mrs. Jefferson had draped her coat over him.

"Wish I'd a thought first to bring some blankets. Lawd! How'd I come way down here without thinkin' 'bout how cold yall had to be? And without no car, too. But I was scared Buford might wake up. He'd think somebody stealin' his automobile. Never learned to drive it, but I *see* how it's done."

Justice and Dorian and Mrs. Jefferson came close around Thomas and Levi. Justice, crouched beside Thomas, kept quiet. They all did.

Thomas smoked a second cigarette sitting there, looking at his brother. He inhaled the smoke deeply and turned his head clear away to let it out. Some of the smoke drifted back down on his brother anyway. Thomas had placed the palm of his right hand on Lee's bare chest under the shirt. At times he stared straight ahead at the tree trunk. His hand on Lee's chest would then become electrified with tremors, and the rest of them would know he was seeing into Lee's vital organs.

It was not essential that Thomas physically touch Levi in order to scan him. But the touching connected the two of them with infeeling. It was not even necessary for them to trace to each other while in *touch*, with Thomas opening the corridor between them as he scanned. They knew how far one felt for and lived in the other. In *touch*, they were not just close. They were one, and one for one, without malice, despair or desperation. They were *brother*; and *brother* was an abiding comfort to himself.

Thomas smiled thoughtfully down on Lee. The same smile, tired but grateful for Thomas, as Thomas was deep down for Lee, smiled back.

"Even if you turn your head," spoken by Dorian, "you still cause him to breathe your smoke.

You can still contaminate his lungs with it. And you ought to stop."

Thomas slowly turned his head to stare at the boy. His look of coldness swept Dorian from head to foot, steely eyes never wavering. It was night out beyond the tree, and heavy darkness within the wet boughs. Yet they could divine the slightest detail of each other. Divining was like seeing through space that had no shine or light to it, and also no darkness. It was a thing opaque through which they knew how to see.

A gentle rain began coming down on the Trace lands.

*Healer?* Thomas traced. He would not speak and risk stuttering. *You ever wonder why you never can quite heal Lee? Ever think about why he stays sick, no matter what you do for him?*

"That's not true," Justice said, breaking in.

*Why don't you let the healer answer?* Thomas traced.

"Because he doesn't know everything I know about it," she said.

Thomas grinned a deadly smile at her. *Quite so. I know what you're going to say. I can read minds, too, you'll remember. You were going to say that making Lee go to the future weakens him, and so much so, it takes away all the healer can do for him. Right?* He didn't wait for an answer.

*But you make him go there anyway, and that's your crime.*

"You read what I want you to read," she said softly.

*I hate your guts*, he traced, with a most dangerous calm.

*I know that. But it doesn't change one thing*, she traced. *You still read what I want you to read.*

*Hope to see you dead, too*, he traced flatly.

*Chil'ren! Believer, this brother and sister!*

*Oh, the hell with you, too*, Thomas traced to the Sensitive. *You make me sicker'n anything, listening in on us.*

Abruptly he grew quiet. He could feel Lee pulling back from him. Only a moment ago they had been *brother*. Now the infeeling let them loose and their fates took on their separate courses. Seeing Lee's look of defeat, Thomas let his anger and his enemies go until the task at hand was finished.

There was silence as Thomas worked. He never told what he found at these times of treatment. He closed his concentration within chambers of cold so that even Justice would have difficulty getting through. For he would find again what he had found before. There was no doubt. Lee's was a grave illness which, in normal humans, grew progressively worse. Its most obvious symptoms were weakness, fatigue and weight loss. Heavy bleeding might occur from superficial wounds. Thomas discovered that Lee's liver had become enlarged.

He sighed. Removed his hand from Lee. "D-Dorian," he said, his voice catching in his throat. He did not care that he stuttered. "N-need him t-t-to p-prod-duce theee c-cure," he said. "A-all of y-you b-besst con-concen-t-trate on thee abb-d-domen." *Justice, if you would transfer the Watcher . . .*

"But I can't do that."

*You mean, you won't do it, not even for Lee,* Thomas traced.

Once Justice transferred the Watcher to Dorian, she had no power over It, in the sense that if she willed It, It would will out. She wasn't at all certain she *could* transfer It, since It was a condition of her mutant genetic material.

Finally she said, "We'll use the Watcher through me. Since It's the power of light, what we have to do is focus It to the right wavelength. Then Dorian will use his healant within the light."

"You transfer the healant to the light," Levi said, agreeing with Justice. "The healant will radiate with the X-rays."

"Or we could become the unit again and use the Watcher through all of us," she said.

"Y-y-youu c-can't d-do that," Thomas said. "Y-youu want t-to k-k-k-ill him?"

"Hush now!" Mrs. Jefferson said. "Talkin' in front of him that way—the idea!"

*Look, spirit woman, he's my brother*, Thomas traced, *and I'll say what I want to. And you are nothing, so keep out of it.*

Levi had hold of Thomas' arm and knew he was tracing meanly to the Sensitive.

"Please . . . I want to get . . . home."

Thomas looked worried. *Sorry. Really, I'm sorry, Lee*, he traced. He crawled from under the tree, turning his back on them. *Let Justice do it. She's got the power* down. He moved off toward the Quinella River.

*We need you here*, Justice telepathed to him. *You know Levi needs you close.*

*I can do it from over here. I can concentrate just as well from right here.*

Levi lifted his head, looking all around him. "Tom-Tom? Tom-Tom, come back."

*I'm right over here, Lee. Just go on with it. Lay back down. I'll be right here.*

"Cruel, that's all it is," whispered Mrs. Jefferson under her breath. "Ought to be downright ashamed. And be his brother wantin', too."

"Let's get on with it," Justice said. "We'll use the Watcher through me, focusing the light the way you first taught Dorian and me, Mrs. Jefferson."

"Why, certainly, Justice chile," Mrs. Jefferson said. "I be right here for you if and when you need me."

"Right," Justice said, and began to trace, *Dorian, be ready.*

Dorian was very still. He concentrated his power at once. They all concentrated, fixing their sensory on Levi's abdomen. They sensed Levi gathering their strength to him, as well as whatever was left of his own strength. He managed an encouraging smile before Justice began. Then Levi turned his head away, unwilling to witness his sister's transmutation.

For Justice was about to change. The change had first started the moment the Watcher had revealed Itself. And a subtle transformation of her continued whenever the Watcher was called upon. By now the change had reached her surface qualities, where it appeared to have altered the skeletal structure of her head. Bones enclosing the brain in the solid box of the cranium seemed to have shifted in the formation of the eyesockets. Justice's forehead appeared longer; her ears were smaller.

At the times of the Watcher, those around her felt they might touch her awesome power. Its effect on them was such that they couldn't quite grasp that she was forever different; yet they knew she was, knew that what was happening was real.

That was why Levi turned away. He could not bring together such a divine process there under the tree with the down-to-earth around him. It was too much to comprehend that Justice of the Watcher was thousands of years apart from them. He wondered where it would all end. And closed his eyes, unwilling even to attempt to see so far into the depths of time.

The gloaming of the Watcher came through pinpoints in Justice's eyes. Dorian's hands on Levi glowed before the ghostly bones of them became visible as the X-rays passed through his tissue. He administered the healant and it flowed with the rays through Levi.

Their concentration, the Watcher and the healant, were at work for no longer than a moment or two. Then the Watcher dimmed and vanished.

"Done," Justice said, breaking the spell of unearthliness that had surrounded them like a mist.

Slowly, Levi turned to them. He saw Justice and was glad her alteration was no longer so pronounced. But he knew, as they all did, that the change was permanent, although gradual. They couldn't tell how much of it was normal development and how much was not. They didn't want to know; they had had no time to prepare themselves. They didn't want to think about it now.

Swiftly, Justice read their denials and their wish not to know. She was alone in her difference. In her growing solitude. She said nothing, keeping her attention on her brother.

He began stirring back to life, as it were. In fifteen minutes they were helping him to his feet and out from under the tree. He stood there in the open, looking all around him. Strength came to him from air and earth. He grew stronger before their eyes.

"Careful when you move," Justice told him. "Remember the snake beds. Ready to go?"

"Ready as I'm gonna be," he said.

They started out. All was quiet. They went single file through the field of weeds that led to the winding Quinella Road. No matter that the field was wet; they were already soaked to the bone.

They climbed through the barbed-wire fence of the field one at a time, each helping the others. And made it to the road. They stood there in a bunch, savoring the road's hard surface, no dust anywhere. In one day and one night the future had given them up to the past, which at last became the present.

No one said it, but they all were thankful to be where they were. And now they moved on, homeward bound.

## 11

They all carried their shoes, even Mrs. Jefferson.
The Sensitive walked beside her son, swinging her
Mexican huaraches. The huarache sandals were
made of woven leather strips that smelled to
heaven when they got wet. Mrs. Jefferson waved
the huaraches around so everyone could get a good
whiff.

"Ain't that somethin'? Hee, hee, hee," she
laughed.

*That's rank*, Thomas traced, moving away from
her.

"Bet nothin' in the future smell like them of
my shoes," she said.

"I don't remember smelling many different
smells there," Dorian said.

"W-welll, I d-do," Thomas said darkly. And
had a clear vision of far-off, filthy Slakers.

Justice had her mind on the road. The hard
feel of the blacktop surface deserved her full at-

tention. The pavement was still warm from the day's blistering heat and felt deliciously wet under her toes. Moisture steamed up from it like ghostly breaths. The whole night was thoroughly warm. It had dark fluffs of cloud with sudden rushes of wind, and a moon blinking on and off. This had to be the best night in all of their lives, she thought. They had returned.

She, along with Thomas, entertained on the long, exhilarating homeward hike, while Levi pondered the future's whereabouts.

On a steep turn of the winding road Thomas planted a McDonald's with its golden arches, and with cars pulling up, full of happy teenagers. Astonished, Justice and the others laughed, then applauded loudly. They groaned as the bright and perfect illusion faded away in the darkness. Kindly Thomas did leave them with the mouth-watering aroma of Big Macs.

"No kidding, man," Dorian said, "couldn't we stop off at the chicken place on the way home? I'm so hungry. I ain't eaten in a million years!"

They burst out laughing again, for it could have been true, considering where they had just been.

"What'll we do for money?" Justice asked him.

"Mom, did you bring any?" Dorian asked, then noticed his mother wasn't carrying a pocketbook.

"I never thought once . . ." she said. "Bet it ain't open this time of night, that chicken place—

no way. But the truck stop, the Grill, now it's most likely open still. About a mile out of the way, though."

"Hey, man!" Dorian said to Thomas. "You could make up the money! Just give the dude some green *magic*. Let him put *that* in his cashbox. He won't know it's gonna fade."

Again they laughed. Except for Thomas.

Justice glanced at him. She knew he hadn't once considered using illusions in that way until now. And now he would think about never using real money again. She would have to give him a counter-suggestion deep within the fabric of his mind; she was quick to shield the thought from him.

At the very top of the final Quinella Road hill, the B&O Railroad tracks cut across the road like two silver scars. Beyond these tracks was Morrey Street, running parallel to the tracks where the Quinella Road came to an end. They would travel Morrey to Tyler Street, which would take them clear across town.

Ten minutes later they reached the top of the hill. Justice projected an image there on the night. Sitting on the tracks and blocking the entire end of the Quinella Road appeared an image of a huge Justice smiling up at the stars. Her head alone was twenty feet high on massive shoulders that dwarfed the tangle of forest trees on either side.

They could see her face shining up there as clearly as they saw the moon caught in the black ripples of her curly hair. Hair like an ocean now.

"Wow!" Dorian said. "Wow-weee!"

The Justice projection was something like watching a movie screen. Unlike one of Thomas' illusions that beclouded their minds, which they accepted as absolutely real—no question—this was a picture of something, definitely, and an entertainment.

"Justice Grown Very Large," Levi said.

Justice grinned, admiring her own handiwork. They paused at the foot of the image as it looked down and smiled on each one of them.

"Goodness gracious," Mrs. Jefferson said, "that's real pretty, isn't it?"

Thomas couldn't help adding to the Justice projection. All at once tiny arrows zipped around the image's head. They pierced the Justice's ears and nose and turned into golden rings.

"Oh, you, Thomas!" Justice told him, only mildly angry with him.

It was a mystery how, just then, two hands reached out of the night and plucked at the outline of Justice's image. The hands pulled the image out, as thread is pulled from a hem. The hands neatly tied the outline in a large silver bow.

They oohed and ahhed, laughed and applauded as, grandly, Thomas bowed to the ground.

"You are *great* at it," Justice told him, "no doubt about that."

*I'm the master*, he traced.

They heard a car coming up the road. Turning behind them, they saw its headlights coming on. They all bunched close to Thomas as he planted magic trees around them. It wouldn't do for someone to come upon them in the dead of night so far from town. The car slid past them, unable to see through the make-believe trees, in which, for some odd reason, Thomas had placed gray monkeys leaping from branch to branch.

"We best hurry," said the Sensitive, " 'fore we wake some folks up or somethin'. Cause some wonder."

"There's no one around here," Levi said. "Thomas wouldn't let anyone see us. And anyhow the fresh air is just fine."

*You feel okay?* Thomas traced to him.

"I'm okay, really. I'm feeling better every minute," Levi said.

Justice hung on his shoulder, the way she had done before, when they'd been merely brother and sister and not ones of power. Levi let her pull on him in this way, although he had not much strength for her added weight. He liked being near her. She was always so open and honest with him. He knew they must return to the future, to solve the riddle of Dustland.

"Glad you feel good," Justice told him. Then she folded her arms with her shoes against her chest and walked with him as before.

Thomas walked in front of her and Levi and behind Dorian and the Sensitive. He kept his hands in his pockets. He had tied the laces of his shoes together and slung them around his neck. The way he hunched his shoulders and his hands thrust in his pockets made him seem older, more mature than Justice or Dorian or Levi.

Well, we're all older, aren't we? Justice thought. Silly to think we could be the same as we were even a few days ago, after what we've seen and done.

But Thomas did seem to her to be at least ten years older now than his twin brother. She thought of reading him. She could do this as swiftly as she could close off her own mind from any probe. But rarely would she read Thomas, not unless she had a suspicion he was controlling Levi. She felt that his mind was rightfully his own, as Lee's was privately his and Dorian's his. Yet she was curious about all those troubling and mixed emotions Thomas had. One moment he could hate so hard. The next, he would be so considerate of his brother. Justice never knew when to suspect him, which kept her constantly on the alert for trouble.

Probably he doesn't know how he'll act either, she thought. That sure would keep him on edge, too. 'Course, he resents me. Oh, admit it, he *hates* me. Thomas, my brother, my own flesh and blood, hates me to death!

The thought made her cringe. It hurt her and made her feel sad. She took a deep breath and let it out slowly.

He'd like me all right if I didn't make him go to the future, she went on to herself. But we just have to go back. I mean, go forward—isn't it?

As though guessing what was in her mind, Levi started talking about the future.

"Have any of you thought about *where* it is?" he asked them.

"No," Dorian said, for all of them.

Thomas shrugged, turning to glance around at Lee.

"What I mean," Levi went on, "when you talk about *in the future* or a hundred years from *now*, you have to be thinking they are a good ways off, that they are far away."

"True," Justice said. "To me, the future, at least the Dustland future, is a far-distant place."

"You agree with that, Tom-Tom?" Levi said.

*Well, for the sake of whatever you're playin' around with*, Thomas traced, agreeing. He nodded.

"No kidding," Levi said. "Don't you think of the present as here and now and the future as something like then and there?"

Thomas nodded. *I guess so.* He kept on walking his easy, yet careful gait, as if he were strolling through an unfamiliar park.

"So the future is far away and a long time to come," said Levi, "just as the past is a long time ago and far away in the opposite direction."

*I'll accept that as an accurate definition of future and past*, Thomas traced.

"Okay, then," Levi said. "But you know . . . *we* didn't go *anywhere*. Where could even our minds go? We—us with our minds—stayed in the same place. The future was right there at the Quinella. Our thoughts didn't go to the future. The Crossover has to be in our heads, right in front of our eyes at that river."

"Wh-what's yourrr p-point?" Thomas asked impatiently.

"The point being," Levi said, "that all of it, every single bit of it, happened *behind* our eyes. *Inside* our heads. It's all inside us. Our minds didn't go anywhere!"

Silence. Thomas stopped, looking down at Morrey Street, on which they were now walking. Then he moved on again. *No*, he traced.

"Why not?" Lee asked him.

Suddenly, Justice said, "I agree with Thomas. It has to be no."

"You, Dorian?" Levi asked.

Dorian nodded. "Yeah. I mean, no, I don't

think the future is inside us. You know, Dustland in our minds, inside us."

"Because," Justice said, "the present isn't just in our minds. The present is us right on this road, is under us, over us, all around us, *and* we keep it in mind. Yet, it's really here," pointing around them. "We can see it and feel it. Hear it. Also, we can think about it."

"But that's it!" Levi said. "Hey, I want to ask you some questions," he said to Justice. "And you please answer 'my mind' to each of them."

"My mind?" she said. "Is this some test?"

"Just do it, please?" he asked.

"Okay."

Levi said, "Justice, what do you see with?"

"You want me to start now?" she asked.

"Yes! What do you see with?"

"My mind."

"And what do you feel and hear with and smell with? And project images with?"

"My mind."

"So," he said. He was quiet a moment.

"Is that it?" Justice wanted to know. "Do I say 'my mind' anymore?"

"No, that's it," Lee said quietly, and then: "Everything we know about anything comes through our senses. Which is another way of saying it comes through our minds. It's our minds that control our senses. So we can't get outside of our minds. We can't *know* that we haven't made up everything we feel and hear and smell about the future. We could have just made it all up, the way Justice made up that huge image of herself up in the sky."

*Oh, I get it now,* Thomas traced to all of them. *Justice, you remember when Mom was taking some course and she'd come home with these mental games, mind gymnastics?*

"Yes," Justice said. "She wanted to know if a tree fell in a forest and no one saw it or heard it, did it actually fall, or something."

*Right,* he traced. *But I believe, just because we only know with our minds doesn't mean that we don't know the truth. That we don't know what we're seeing. I mean, we all see a tree is a tree and not some bloody frog . . . and I'm not talking about projections or illusions, either. They're something altogether else.*

"The future has to be another dimension," Justice said. "We found a way of uncovering it. I think it surrounds us, just like now surrounds us when we're here. If this were the future, we'd be strolling through Dustland. And we have to cross over to get to it. We have to *bridge* time. Because to live like we're living now is to be *in* time. We're right here *taking* our time."

"It's too neat," Levi said.

*Not any neater than your way*, Thomas traced.
*But what does it matter? We'll probably never know
where the future is. It just is, and we get to it,
that's all I know. I know bloody well I was there.
I sure as hell do! Miacis, blah!* He laughed scorn-
fully. *Them awful-looking winged things.* Meaning
Slakers. He had certainly gotten his hate up over
the Bambnua and her crew, Justice realized.

"What's he talkin' 'bout?" Mrs. Jefferson
asked them.

Their minds verged as Justice informed the
Sensitive, through tracing, all that had transpired
with the Slakers before the Roller and Miacis
brought Thomas and Levi back again. It was news
to the two boys as well.

"We didn't have time to tell you before we left
there," Justice told them. "I think it won't matter
what Slakers look like, or whether they die out
sometime farther along in the future. What matters is that they get a free chance to see what they
can do."

"Mercy!" cried Mrs. Jefferson. "All that goin'
on—must take all your strength just to keep it
straight. Thinkin' about it and even been in it!"

"That's why we have to rest," Justice said.
"And a good long time." She glanced through the
dark at Levi, seeing him in the opaqueness of
sensory. "Time to study the Crossover and its dan-
gers," she said. "And all the wrong things about

Dustland." But that's only the beginning, she thought to herself.

*Oh, take your time*, traced Thomas. The tracings quivered with sarcasm. *Have all the time you need. Have a good time at it.*

They fell silent, knowing how much Thomas hated his predicament. They did feel for him; but they would not stop what Justice had to do.

Are we slaves to her? Levi wondered. It was so sudden a thought, with not an inkling that it was coming. He shuddered in shock at the very idea.

We go there because we are the first unit. We have to go, to do whatever the first unit must do.

That calmed him. And all the way across town on Tyler Street, he trudged undisturbed.

Their bare feet made no sound on the street. There were absolutely no cars moving in the middle of the night. And yet they were fearful they might be seen. Houses were dark, but an occasional porch light had been left on by some forgetful homeowner. Thomas let a mist surround them, a kind of dark mist, not unlike the darkness in the melancholy corners of his mind. But he was tired, exhausted clear through by their ordeal. Often as not, his mist faded away. But cars parked at curbs and shiny with wet did much to block the view of them from houses.

What happened when they were at the end of

Tyler and ready to cross Dayton Street on the short distance home occurred without warning. There was not an inkling that anything unlikely was coming, just as there had been no inkling of Levi's shocking thought that they all could be slaves to Justice.

Only she was given a fraction of an instant's clairvoyance, in which the glow of the Watcher was there in her eyes. She traced, screaming: DIVE! DIVE!

On pure reflex, they dove to the ground, shoes flying every which way. Justice knocked Levi down with her. Thomas and Dorian dived to either side of them, at once locking hands across their backs. Somehow Justice and Levi caught hold of Thomas' and Dorian's free hands. In two seconds the four of them were joined. They were the first unit and power, immense with light.

An unspeakable, malevolent sweep of something deadly came out of the future. It hovered unbearably above them. It swept by, reversed itself and swept over them again. Then it went on, out of the present, back from whence it came.

It had Mrs. Jefferson, who hadn't been quick enough. Caught her mind in its dreadful, relentless will and carried it away.

But the unit was present and power. It was the Watcher and knowing. It overtook the sweep at the edge of time-present. It had no moment to study whatever it was that was malevolent and yet was wise with the wisdom of time. The thing was energy, blind energy, light's darkest side, if that were possible. There was no moment to wonder what could come out of the future, the way the first unit had gone to it. The unit would perhaps study that later. Now it wanted only the Sensitive. It would not permit her or anything to be taken from the present.

The unit did not win Mrs. Jefferson back by its superior power. It was rather more like the Malevolence handed her over. As if saying, "Here, you want her? You can have her. She got in the way. It was you we came to find."

The unit brought back her mind. But such frenzy had jarred her senses; she was knocked out, flat on the ground.

After the sweep had gone, having found what it had been searching for, the four of them released one another's hands. They found their shoes scattered over the dark street. After a time Mrs. Jefferson came to, although feeling numbed still.

"What have we done?" she whispered to Justice. "Baby-girl, what have we brought forth!"

"Here, you got yourself all muddy," Justice said, trying to brush her off. They helped Mrs. Jefferson to her feet.

"Listen," Justice said, "whatever came looking for us left when it found us. It could have hurt us, could have taken any one of us, I guess, if it could take Mrs. Jefferson. Probably couldn't take the unit—though I'm not sure of that."

"It . . . it came from the future," Levi said. He was shaking with fear. The thing's power of ill-will gave him the worst feeling.

"It must've come from somewhere beyond Dustland," Justice said.

"So." It was Thomas. He gazed into Justice's eyes. He knew now what an enemy really was; or, at least, where to find it. It was not Justice.

*Dustland*, he traced. *Dustland's a bloody zoo!* Letting them all in on the tracing.

"No." Quietly she answered him. They stood together at the side of the street. Steam rose around them, ghostly warm from the cooling pavement. She could look over beyond Dayton Street to the Union Road, where her dear home was hidden by trees. Only a little longer now and they would be home.

"What came after us doesn't want us disturbing things," she said. "I wonder if all in Dustland are caught by it, including Miacis. Poor, beautiful Miacis! Poor Slakers, and worlmas, too. Dustland's a prison."

*Yes! I can see that now*, Thomas traced. *Worse than any zoo!*

"Oh, boy," Levi said, like a moan.

There was utter quiet in which each of them

sensed separately, probing the night with their different abilities. They had a moment to think about all they knew and had guessed and wondered about Dustland.

Whatever was here is gone now," Mrs. Jefferson said. "But it haunts me—mercy, it haunts me still!"

With that, she put her arm through Dorian's. Without another word, she and her son passed along Dayton Street to their home. Justice and her brothers quickly crossed to the Union Road, which dead-ended at their own house.

Soundlessly they came up on the dark lane leading to the house and passed beneath branches of an enormous cottonwood tree. It was the property's sentinel, the tree which for many years Justice had called Cottonwoman.

Grand old woman, you! Sensing now that the tree would forever be her friend.

Take off that shawl, Cottonwoman. But keep your bonnet on. The night's too warm for covers, and the rain may come again.

High up, the cottonwood tree caught the wind. Leaves whooshed and rustled, sounding to Justice as though the tree laughed heartily in agreement with her.

# 12

They eased up on the dark house and put their shoes back on. They stood there, unmoving, probing all the rooms. They did this not out of fear but from what was becoming habit. Since their visits to Dustland they'd become wary of houses, or doors that could close them in. Justice and her brothers distrusted all enclosures. However, they uncovered nothing sinister in their sweet old home. Their mom was revealed stretched out on the couch in the parlor in a dark blue nightgown and robe. Mrs. Douglass had folded her hands along the side of her face. Sound asleep, she looked relaxed, except for a slight frown caught in the curve of one eyebrow.

Mother. My pretty mommy, thought Justice.

She felt a pang of love to see her mother so.

If I could change things, I would change it all, Justice thought.

Mr. Douglass was also asleep. He had nodded

off in his easy chair next to the couch. There was no evidence that he had been reading. The floor lamp at the side of the chair was not on. There were no newspapers fallen at his feet. He'd simply been sitting there for half the night. Perhaps thinking. Wondering if and when his children—what could he call them now?—would ever return.

Justice's folks knew that when the three of them unexpectedly disappeared, they had gone to the future. No matter how incredible the idea seemed, they knew the truth of it. But this was the first time the three of them had been gone all day and night. Clearly, her folks had worried themselves sick.

With power of mind, Justice unlocked the front door and opened it. They walked easily within the house they loved.

The instant they crossed the threshold of the parlor, Mr. Douglass was wide awake and turning on the light behind him. He stared at his children, snagged his vision on Justice's altering features and quickly looked down. The three of them stood attentive, calm, not saying anything until Levi crossed the room and shook his mother by the shoulder.

"Mom. Mom," he said, "we're home."

Mrs. Douglass was a long moment coming awake. They watched as layers of sleep lifted from her. But all at once she recognized Levi. And shoved him away in revulsion. She caught herself, leaped up to make amends. She stepped on her gown, tripped and would have fallen if Mr. Douglass hadn't been there in time to catch her.

She had seen Justice at the moment she stepped wrong. And it took Mr. Douglass and both his sons holding on to her to calm her.

Slowly, Justice came forward, keeping her face hidden behind her father's back. She reached around, gently touched her mother's hair.

"Sorry," Justice mumbled. She couldn't think to say more, so full was she with love, with regret. She stepped back away from them.

More than once she had thought about using the power they had to ease some of the pain of their parents' having children like themselves. She knew well that, for her folks, her gift of extra-sensory was a terrifying affliction. The fact that all of their children were afflicted with the same defect was almost beyond bearing. Often as not, Justice and her brothers responded to their folks like normal young people on the verge of growing up. They admired their parents greatly and had no will to use the power on them.

Now Justice did what she knew she must do— bring the terror into the open in the hope that with familiarity it would seem less horrible. She let be what she could not help becoming. The Watcher came into her eyes.

Using no voice or gesture, she presented the power to their minds. Respectfully the Watcher revealed to them all that they had seen and done in Dustland, and what had happened in the Crossover. It made clear the presence of the Malevolence, the thing that had searched them out, here in the present.

It will come again, the Watcher informed. Mal has found its way and it will sweep. It will come. Mal comes to strike fear so that first unit will not return to Dustland. The first unit will return. The end of Dustland is only the beginning for first unit. I am the Watcher. I know.

The Watcher faded. Justice appeared both shapeless and all angles at once. In the artificial light, her eyes were too small, eyesockets too large. Her folks turned away every other moment, as if the Watcher's light still glowed, hurting them. She knew it was the alteration that caused them to turn. They would imagine it greater than it was. And she thought of something that might make things easier for them.

"I'd change anyway when I was older," she told them, sounding normal and young. "I mean, five years from now I wouldn't look the same as I do today. I'd be taller and better developed. My face, my features would change on their own." Of course, what she was saying was true.

"L-l-let her h-hair gr-gr-ow out," Thomas told

them, "annnd you-you w-on't even n-n-notice how h-herrr nnneck has th-th-inned." Pull it down around her cheeks, he thought, maybe get her some tinted glasses . . . some dark sunglasses.

He knew well that he could cloud the minds of outsiders so they saw Justice as normal. It was his parents he would protect from seeing her alter before their eyes.

They stayed in the room, all of them standing, for some time. Carefully, quietly, the children persuaded Mr. and Mrs. Douglass that, even with their power, much about them remained the same. Indeed, Thomas was still the wild and moody, thoughtless one.

My drums! Thomas thought suddenly. Man, I forgot all about them! Full of excitement, he remembered his drums were there in his room. Thomas was a master at the tympani and a fine drummer, too.

Levi remained the sensitive one. "I feel better today than I've felt for a long time," he told them.

"Have you felt ill, then?" his father asked.

"No," Levi lied, "I just feel very, very good now."

He was the one who liked most listening to symphony through the earphones of his hi-fi. He was most kind to Justice. But he would no longer write his poetry and stories in secret, he had decided. He would let Justice read them, if she liked.

The greatest change had come to Justice. The physical alteration, although subtle, was undeniable. And she appeared unaccountably taller, as tall as Thomas and Levi. She could not quite return to the carefree, energetic young person she had been only a month or two ago. Those seeing her were gripped by the intelligence in her eyes even when the Watcher wasn't present. And yet there were moments when she acted just like a kid; walked and talked like a kid. These came when for hours she forgot about the future, when she was caught up again in the long, hot days of late summer in the town.

They cajoled their folks into accepting their condition. It was Mr. Douglass who managed best to put it aside. It was simple faith he had in them, in what he knew them to have been before their power; and he held on to that. He and his wife were powerless to assist them in whatever they must do to untangle themselves from their present dilemma.

Mr. Douglass let go of his anguish in the gesture of his hand smoothing back his hair. He had dark circles under his eyes. His wife was sobbing again into her hands. She did that often. He did, too. The tears would come to either one of them at any time with the suddenness of a dam breaking. He accepted the tears as a way of relieving the steady tension of their days. And he would have been comforted to know that the children also cried.

"You all must be starved," he said to them.

Pieces of their family life seemed to fall into place.

"We're about starved to death," Levi said, and felt a ravaging hunger atop his exhaustion. He stumbled over to sit in the easy chair his dad had just vacated.

Mrs. Douglass let her hands fall from her face. They could see that her eyes were dry. No more tears would come.

"We'll get the bacon started," Mr. Douglass said. He took his wife gently by the arm.

"Oh, boy!" Levi said. "Want some help?"

"No!" Mrs. Douglass said, too quickly, the first word she'd spoken. It was so like Lee to offer help faster than Justice or Tom-Tom. "I'll make the eggs," she managed, her voice hoarse and whispery.

"I'll make pancakes!" Lee announced.

"No! No!"

What more was there to say? Mr. Douglass hurried her from the room. In a moment she was back. "You'll have to be patient with me," she said softly. She looked each one of them straight in the eyes, turned and left the room.

The three of them visibly relaxed once she was gone. No need to talk. Thomas opened the corridor between his and Levi's minds.

*Let's go to our room*, he traced to Lee.

*I feel I could sleep for a year*, Lee traced back.

*You mind if I drum?*

*It'll be like music to my ears*, Lee traced. *Make all the rhythms you want to.*

*Thanks.*

*Justice*, Thomas traced, *we're going in.*

*But don't go to sleep*, she traced back. *Breakfast will be ready in a half-hour or so.*

*I was going to sleep*, Levi traced. *How could I forget that quick? I really must be tired.*

*You can sleep*, Thomas traced. *I'll wake you.*

*I'm going, too*, Justice said, getting up. *Thomas, give me a knock when it's time, will you?*

She went to her room as the boys went to theirs, closing the door behind her. Seeing her dear room caused a sob to escape her. It was usually a mess from her hurry to be everywhere at once. But now it was neat as a pin. She grinned. Her mom had bought her a pile of new paperback books and had left them neatly by her pillow. Justice hugged the books to her. Oh, it would be great reading every one of them. Well, not in the daytime when there was so much to see and do. But at night; at night, reading them one after another, she thought.

If I want to stay up half the night, I will, too. And use the Watcher to read by.

That gave her the giggles. But she sobered quickly.

No. No, never play with the power. Use Levi's flashlight to read by.

She fell asleep on top of the books. She slept until Levi poked his head in. Thomas hadn't been decent enough to wake her after all.

"We're at the table," Levi told her. "Better hurry. Don't even wash up."

"But I have to," she said. She rushed off to the bathroom, where she splashed handfuls of soapy water on her face and neck. Drying herself, she stared into the mirror at the Justice she had become. She looked carefully. It was so difficult for her to see the surface of things. But soon a view of her own changing was visible to her and not at all shocking. For she was aware of her changing within as well. She felt no imbalance, no alienness. That would mean that her mind was completely atuned to the alteration. And there were times now when she felt that her skin and muscle, her bone and marrow, encased her in a tube. She didn't at all like the feeling. Less and less did she like the weight of herself.

Never bothered me once, she thought, until the time I was within the mind of the Bambnua. She was so heavy. And I was so *light*.

She hurried out, through the parlor and down the hall to the kitchen, where all of them were seated. She plopped down between her mom and dad, the two boys across from them. She ignored Thomas, since he hadn't waked her. She noted that they were eating in the kitchen rather than the dining room, the place they ate on special occasions. That was a good sign.

"Isn't it funny to be having breakfast in the middle of the night?" she asked.

"Funnier than two fleas drowning in a buttercup," her dad said amiably. "Now dig in. Don't stand on ceremony, for you know how ceremony can't stand to be stood on."

"Ho!" giggled Justice, and served herself a pile of bacon and some scrambled eggs.

"Trying to make your plate disappear," her dad said.

"Ummmm," was about the only sound she could make with her mouth full. She quickly gobbled the eggs so she could fit pancakes with butter and syrup dripping all over them where the eggs had been.

"Oh, brother," she finally was able to say, "I'm gonna faint at the sight!"

No one fainted, but it was not possible that three kids, even when two of them were teenagers, could eat so much so fast.

"Oh, my stomach," Levi moaned, but he

wouldn't stop eating. None of them did, until every scrap of toast, of eggs and bacon and pancakes was gone.

Mr. Douglass looked stunned by their appetites. Mrs. Douglass was delighted at seeing her kids were as normal and as hungry as other kids. She made them more pancakes. They ate them while their folks drank coffee and picked at the toast Mrs. Douglass had just made.

You could sure see *they* hadn't been on a long journey for a day and a night, Justice noted.

"We drank a whole quart of orange juice," Justice said.

Justice and her brothers began talking about the journey. They speculated about it until one of them noticed that it was morning, that the sun was up to heat the day to sweltering again. Oh, fantastic July! With just your normal everyday 1980s dust in the air, along with birds and clouds and ninety degrees!

Again they talked of the future, easing it into the conversation without a second thought. They talked again of t'beings and Slakers and Thomas' grand illusions. But no one told how Tom-Tom had run away just to spite Justice. They kept the struggle between Justice and Thomas to themselves. Maybe, with the coming of Malevolence, that had changed.

Mr. and Mrs. Douglass suspected something

about Thomas. As he talked on and on, the more they realized how unkind he could be and how stealthy and improper was his train of thought.

He told them he could get them anything they needed to live, that neither of them need ever work again. "G-get wh-what I w-w-want f-f-for f-f-free," he stuttered.

"Thomas," Justice said. But nothing could stop him once he'd got going on his masterful illusions.

Until Mr. and Mrs. Douglass drew into themselves, away from their children. Mr. Douglass encircled his wife in his arms protectively. She cringed tightly against him.

Just when everything was going so well, Justice thought.

Her folks wouldn't look at them. They had pulled into themselves, where they might still find some safety.

Finally Thomas noticed and left off.

*You're a first-class idiot*, Justice traced to him.

*Look, I was only trying to get them good and relaxed. But they act like we're some freaks!*

*You never understand anything*, Justice traced.

*Well*, you *sure know it all!*

"We'd better get some sleep," she said, breaking the silence at the table.

Mr. Douglass loosened his hold on his wife. She straightened in her chair, but did not look up.

Justice knew not to offer to do the dishes, and she traced a warning to Levi not to offer his help. They'd best retreat now. She hoped that she and her brothers would always be able to come back home. And for the first time she seriously wondered whether they'd always be welcome.

The three of them slept a deep and soundless sleep. Justice slept longest. It was well past noon when she awoke to the tinny, chim/chi-chim, chim/chi-chim of Thomas' standing cymbals.

Oh, my goodness! she thought. It felt like years since she had heard her brother's steady rhythms. She appreciated his cymbals much more than she did his set of drums. Cymbals had a tantalizing sound. Somehow the sound mixed yellow with the sunlight now streaming into her room. She stretched, yawned at the day so bright and hot outside her window.

"Great," she said. She got up. And without disturbing anyone, she padded down the hall to the bathroom, took a shower and got dressed in her usual attire of jeans and tank top.

Maybe will have to change to shorts, she thought. Let's see how it is.

Justice wandered the property aimlessly, thoroughly preoccupied with the heady sights, sounds and smells of life in the present. In the backyard the garden was growing fine. She picked a big, fat, early-ripened tomato—the only one, too—

right off the vine. Ate it, with its juice escaping down her hand. It was so good.

On the west side of the field they owned, she found the ageless hedgerow that she loved walking through.

"Right where I left it!" she said to herself, kidding. It was her favorite place of all, with the line of century-old trees marching down to the end of the property to the right of Dorian Jefferson's house. Great old branches reached out across the row a few feet above the ground, seeking sunlight. She sat on one of the horizontal branches, making it swing. Not long ago she and Thomas and Levi, with all the other neighborhood kids, had hung containers of garter snakes from the branches. That was when Thomas had invented his Great Snake Race; and, to everyone's eternal surprise, Justice had won it.

And here's the place I first discovered I had something different about me, and that my brothers did, too, she thought.

After a while the cymbals inside the house ceased and the drums began their mighty noise.

Brother, he sure loves booming away, Justice thought of Thomas.

Later Thomas and Levi could be seen wandering around, too. She kept out of their way by hiding in the row. They knew she was there and let her have it to herself.

Thomas telepathed to her a mean thought just to get her goat: *Cut down them trees for firewood*.

*Osage orange trees won't burn*, Justice 'pathed to him, *you dumb, stupid dummy!* With anger she hadn't known she was feeling.

*Aw, I was only kidding you. Don't get upset.*

Justice let it go, mildly surprised at his near-apology. While in the row, she started reading one of the books her mom had got her. The book was about dragons and princely knights. It made her laugh; it didn't take her breath away as it would have if she hadn't gone *away* and come back.

By evening Thomas and Levi had wrestled a four-wheeled dolly with Thomas' kettledrums on it out of the house, down the backyard and into the field. They and the neighborhood boys met in the field practically every night.

All of them boys, Justice thought. Who cares?

But she couldn't help going to see what Thomas was up to, and to see all the boys again, Dorian included. It felt like she hadn't seen the kids in years, and she knew it felt the same for her brothers. Earlier in the day all three of them had resisted running off to find everyone. The kids would have simply forgotten about them from the moment at dawn when they'd left for the future. Mrs. Jefferson would've seen to that—not hypnotizing the kids, but suggesting to an area of their memories that Thomas, Justice, Levi and Dorian did not exist.

The deep and rolling tone of the kettles was the key that would unlock their memories again.

An hour after suppertime the neighborhood seemed deserted. The hedgerow, twisted by hard weather, spread early-evening shade across the Douglass field. Levi, Thomas and Justice stood in separate pools of dappled light.

Thomas, clutching four felt-tip mallets, two in each hand, struck them on the calfskin drumheads of the kettles. There commenced a low, trembling sound. It began to build into a bass roar that rolled down the field and on through the hedges of backyards to hit the rear window screens of houses. So much sound was almost visible, bouncing away and sailing over front lawns to slide smoothly into Dayton Street.

As if on cue, Dorian Jefferson slammed out of the back door of his house, sprinted across his backyard, took his back hedge in one perfect low-hurdle stretch-step and bounded into the field on both feet. Standing.

"Sweet!" hollered Thomas, still drumming. "Perfect hurdle, man!"

Dorian grinned from ear to ear. A compliment from Thomas! He'd been waiting practically the whole day for some sign of life from the Douglass house. He knew better than to make a move over there until the three kids were ready and until Mr. and Mrs. Douglass had settled down some.

Running, Dorian zigged and zagged his way up the field. He confronted the three with his dirty-faced, ragged self, still grinning. They all slapped palms. Thomas put his sticks down long enough to do so. No one thought about being the unit. In the field they were simply friends. Thomas started up again; the field boomed and crashed, shaking startled birds out of the trees.

Other boys appeared, as though by signal. Thomas greeted them with rushing swells and rolls of beats as they came off the street and through backyards. There was a kid named Slick Peru, and Danny Grier, who was Thomas' drum teacher's son, and Talley Williams, and a lot of other boys.

Thomas drummed well and acted as if he might be going to drum forever. Justice knew he hadn't called forth the kids just for a drum concert. He loved an audience, though, and he loved inventing games. He'd been drumming when first he invented the Great Snake Race. Also, when drumming, Thomas talked smoothly, and maybe talking smoothly made describing his inventions easier. Justice realized suddenly that in the future Thomas had not stuttered at all. That was because only their minds had been there, she decided; and in his mind Thomas never stuttered.

His drums were humming just loud enough for him to talk above the sound.

"This here's a new game," he began, "of which

I"—Pom-pa-Pom—"the Master Drummer"—
Pom-Pom, Pom-Pom—"am sole inventor and
owner." Pom, Pom pah-pah Pom.

"It is called"—Pom!—"the game"—POM-
POMPOM—"of Dustland!"

Justice did not move a muscle.

"Or Humans versus Slakers!" Pom pah-pah
Pom Pom.

"What are Slakers?" Talley wanted to know.

"Why, buddy," began Thomas, his drums
fairly singing, "Slakers are winged females with
bald pink heads!"

The boys laughed loudly. "Fool!" they said.

"Slakers bomb you from the air with furry
eggs." Pom-ah, Pom-ah.

Boys fell out on the ground.

"But how do you play it?" asked Slick, re-
covering. "What's it called—Dustland?"

"Yea, how do you win it?" somebody else
asked.

"Think of Dungeons and Dragons," Thomas
said, which was a real game that you could buy
and which several of them owned. His drums
rolled. "Each kid has assets and liabilities,
whether human or Slaker. For instance, I, a human, can cloud boys' minds and make you see
whatever I want you to see. I'm called the Illu-
sionist."

Justice found herself grinning. Levi suppressed a laugh.

"What I can't do"—Pom-ma-Pom—"is knock a Slaker out of the sky. But I can cause one to land with my illusion of a crystal lake. Slakers go crazy over fresh water."

"Sounds like fun," said Slick. "But if I want to be a Slaker, how do I learn to fly?"

"How do you become a girl, you mean!" Boys laughed and snickered, much to Justice's disgust.

"Dummy!" Thomas said. Clearly, he had not thought the game through. He would have to start over and change the females to male flyers, which was the way it should be, he thought. He was tired of drumming. He would not risk stuttering by talking. A long look passed between him and Levi, which told Justice that they were tracing. Obviously, Levi was being told what to say through telepathy. The next moment he was making the females wingless.

"It's a game you can do in your living room or on the phone or anywhere. Also, we need some pencils and paper," Levi said. "I'll get some. Each of you decide what you will be, human or Slaker, and what your goods and bads are. You get more points for bads." He avoided looking at Justice.

She was furious. *You know the flyers are women, you know it!* she traced to Thomas.

*Butt out*, he traced back. *This is a game for* guys!

Levi was leaving the field for pencil and paper when it happened, just like before with not an inkling. Except for that split instant of clairvoyance when Justice knew—but there was no time. It had come.

It swept below the grass, coming up the field. Only Thomas, Levi, Justice and Dorian knew it was there. It moved with such swiftness they had not a moment to join. How could they join in front of the boys? But they would have if there had been time, and worried about it later.

Malevolence had swept between the three of them and Dorian. It would not permit the first unit. It made them aware that it had a t'being pinned to its will. It could drop the t'being on the grass if it wanted to. It pretended that it would, but it didn't.

After that, it came each day with dreadful power. Mal came to make sure they were still there and not in the future.

Mrs. Douglass felt herself slipping back into a way of life that she wouldn't have dreamed would be hers ever again. The children had been home over a month now. After that first night, not once had they shown a trace of awesome forces. Thomas never again spoke of getting what he wanted through his illusions. There was no unheard-of glowing in Justice's eyes. If anything, the children were supernormal, going about their daily, lazy summer lives with casual determination. She could almost believe that whatever it was they had, never was. In fact, she decided it was gone and told her husband so.

"They act like anybody else," she told him. "Is it possible we could have imagined it all?"

"June, have you forgotten what happened?" Speaking about the time when the children had revealed their power.

That Mrs. Jefferson creeping into her house.

How could I have been such a fool to leave Justice alone, at the beck and call of that woman? Mrs. Douglass wondered.

Yes, she had been in summer school, and one day she'd come home and it had all begun.

No. Maybe all of it was mass hysteria. They say it happens, she thought. A group of factory workers on an assembly line suddenly see a strange mist and it makes them weak and sick. She'd read about that just recently. Absolutely unexplainable. No escaping gases or anything like that had been detected. And it was mass hysteria attributed to boring, monotonous work. But none in her house worked an assembly line.

Now she and her husband were tidying the kitchen after dinner. She'd finished icing a sheet cake for the kids for when they came back from Thomas' drumming in the field.

"They get along so well," she was saying, turning the cake, admiring it. She knew the children would come in again and again for extra pieces. "Levi has got a sense of humor just like you, have you noticed?"

"June, please. Don't get your hopes up. It's better you consider them forever strangers. It's easier . . . Less pain . . ."

"Oh, for God's sakes!" Furious at him. "My kids are fine, as normal as can be."

"You'd better listen to me," he said. "There's only heartache in wishing it'd go away. It won't! It's real. Nothing will ever be the same. It's here and now! Our kids, our own flesh and blood, are the race to come. They're here . . . first unit!" His voice shaking.

June Douglass spoke in whispered fury: "I don't want to hear about power or Watchers or anything dreadful ever again!"

She stalked out and slammed the door to the bedroom.

She slumbered for what seemed a long time. Through it she was never awake, but she was not quite asleep either. She could still hear Thomas' drums in the field and boys laughing. Once Justice yelling. They were playing some game or other. She heard somebody yell, "Gotta fly! Gotta fly!"

and she was sure a ballgame was going on. Then a long time of nothing, when sound ceased and the evening darkened to night. When she opened her eyes, it was ten-thirty, she saw by the clock on her dresser.

"Well, for . . ." I must have been tired! she thought. She hadn't felt it at all. But she did recall she had been on her feet since early morning, and by evening still busy baking for the—

For a moment Mrs. Douglass couldn't move. Her limbs felt heavy and fragile and she didn't want to move them. If she could just stay in bed, maybe she could hold her world together. But slowly she got up off the bed. Blindly she found the door and hurried down the dark hall. Would not look at open bedroom doors, empty rooms, as she passed them. She would not.

She was out of the house and in the backyard. From the light spilling into the yard from rear windows, she saw Mr. Douglass carefully dollying Thomas' kettledrums through the gate from the field.

He'd covered the drums with a dropcloth to keep moisture off them. He'd stood in the field an hour, listening, hoping, feeling the night slip over him.

He did not look at his wife as he went by her; he struggled with the dolly up onto the porch and into the house. He took the drums into Thomas' and Levi's room. He had his boy's purple hat under his arm. Mrs. Douglass had seen it. She followed him in; when he had finished, he found her seated on the edge of the couch.

He sat himself next to her, taking her hand.

At last she spoke. "Well," she said.

"Yes," he said. She was controlling herself. That was good, he thought.

"When did it happen?" she asked him.

"I was on the screened porch, reading the paper," he said. "The light was going, it got dark; I couldn't see so well and turned on the lamp. Somehow the lamp made me realize how quiet everything was. Even with the riot of birdcalls, there was a kind of stillness. You know how the mockingbirds will sound out before they sleep."

"Yes," she said softly.

"I went on around the house and on out through the backyard to see what was up. And it was over."

"Did you go down to their house?"

"Yes," he said. "His mother was there. But Dorian had gone."

"Yes," she said. "To complete the unit."

"Yes."

They sat there, holding on.

After a time he said, "You have to keep on going, that's all."

"I know," she said.

"They always do come back," he said.

"Do you know where they go to prepare . . ."

"Yes," he said, "but it does no good to know. She wouldn't let us pass."

"I do hate that woman, I can't help myself." Her voice trembled.

"I know," he said. "But there's no need. It comes from them, not Mrs. Jefferson. Actually, it comes from us. We brought them into this world."

"Yes, and why don't *we* have it?"

"Because. It's their time, not ours."

"You mean our human race is done?"

"Just our part of it," he said. "Not all at once. But they are the new order."

She shook her head in denial, yet knew it was true.

After a time she spoke again, her voice trembling now. "Know what the day after tomorrow is?" she asked.

"What?" he said.

"Justice's birthday."

"No! Yes, it sure is!"

"The nineteenth," she said. "She'll be twelve."

"Still a baby," he said. "Twelve."

"Or twelve thousand and ninety-four. Or twelve million!"

"June, don't."

"I ordered a pretty store-bought cake, too, better than I could make it look, just for her. I invited all of the boys and girls, too."

"You mean you already told them?"

"Yep. It was going to be the biggest and best surprise party she ever saw."

He thought a moment. "Well, you can still do it," he said. "They'll be back. They never stay that long."

"I'm so afraid."

"Don't, June. They'll be back, I swear they will. They have always come back."

She stared at him, peered into his eyes as if to discover lies, worries, tricks. It was the worst, most forlorn look he had ever seen. He kept his eyes steady. Thought gentle, easy thoughts, no fear anywhere.

"You promise me they'll come back?" she said. "Promise me my boys? Promise me? Promise me Justice!"

His voice was steady. Power or no, he knew his kids. He smiled. "I promise you," he said.

# ABOUT THE AUTHOR

About the Justice Cycle, author Virginia Hamilton says, "These books introduce readers to siblings who have the extrasensory abilities of telepathy and telekinesis and who are locked in a deadly rivalry in both the present and the future. Moreover, there are well-organized groups in the far future who survive against hopelessly severe odds. Several alien-seeming species of extraordinary beings—human, cyborg, and machine—search for a solution to the desperate conditions."

In *Justice and Her Brothers, Dustland,* and *The Gathering,* powerful, psychic events result in a symbiosis among beings and non-beings alike, and represent a majestic change in what we view as human. "This remarkable development," says Ms. Hamilton, "denotes my belief that change is what is worthy of our effort. The Justice Cycle reveals that the prime certainty we humans have is *uncertainty,* and we'd do well to think about what that means."

Virginia Hamilton is one of the most highly acclaimed writers of our time. She has been awarded the National Book Award, the John Newbery Medal, the Coretta Scott King Award (twice), the *Boston Globe–Horn Book Award* (three times), the Edgar Allan Poe Award, and the Ohioana Book Award (twice). Three of her titles are Newbery Honor Books, including, most recently, HBJ's *In the Beginning: Creation Stories from Around the World.* She and her husband, poet/author Arnold Adoff, live in Ohio.

"Young readers may be so spellbound with this book that they will taste the grit of Dustland for hours or days after the book is finished, but no one can close the book without a sense of being lifted, like the Slaker, beyond the dust into Hamilton's 'enormous world of light.' "

— *The Christian Science Monitor*

## Other books in the Odyssey series:

*L. M. Boston*
☐ THE CHILDREN OF GREEN
   KNOWE
☐ TREASURE OF GREEN KNOWE
☐ THE RIVER AT GREEN KNOWE
☐ AN ENEMY AT GREEN KNOWE
☐ A STRANGER AT GREEN KNOWE

*Edward Eager*
☐ HALF MAGIC
☐ KNIGHT'S CASTLE
☐ MAGIC BY THE LAKE
☐ MAGIC OR NOT?
☐ SEVEN-DAY MAGIC

*Mary Norton*
☐ THE BORROWERS

*John R. Tunis*
☐ THE KID FROM TOMKINSVILLE
☐ WORLD SERIES
☐ ALL-AMERICAN
☐ YEA! WILDCATS!
☐ A CITY FOR LINCOLN

*Virginia Hamilton*
☐ A WHITE ROMANCE
☐ JUSTICE AND HER BROTHERS
☐ DUSTLAND
☐ THE GATHERING

Look for these titles and others in the Odyssey series in your local bookstore.

Or send prepayment in the form of a check or money order to: HBJ (Operator J) 465 S. Lincoln Drive, Troy, Missouri 63379.

Or call: 1-800-543-1918 (ask for Operator J).

☐ I've enclosed my check payable to
   Harcourt Brace Jovanovich.

Charge my: ☐ Visa ☐ MasterCard
          ☐ American Express

_____
**Card Expiration Date**

☐☐☐☐☐☐☐☐☐☐☐☐☐☐☐☐☐☐
**Card #**

_____
**Signature**

_____
**Name**

_____
**Address**

_____
**City**      **State**    **Zip**

Please send me _____
copy/copies @ $3.95 each

($3.95 x no. of copies)  $_____

Subtotal          $_____

Your state sales tax  + $_____

Shipping and handling  + $_____
($1.50 x no. of copies)

Total           $_____

PRICES SUBJECT TO CHANGE